Twelve Below Zero

Anthony Bukoski

Twelve Below

Anthony Bukoski

Zero

Drawings by
Gaylord Schanilec

New Rivers Press 1986

Minnesota Voice Project Number 24

Earlier versions of these stories appeared in the following publications: "True
Adventures" appeared in *Rendezvous*; "Twelve Below Zero" in *Matrix*; "Hello from
Ture" (as "Hello from Thure") in *event*; "The Happiness Farm" in *The Ohio
Journal*; "Ice Days" (as "Nights in Värmland") in *Cut Bank*; "The Kissing Booth" in
The Laurel Review; "Great Sea Battles" in *The Dekalb Literary Arts Journal*; "Harry
and the Dancer" in *The Antigonish Review*; "The Woman Who Ate Cat Food" (as
"In Lenten Season") in *The Davidson Miscellany*; "Route of the Zephyrs" in *The
Crescent Review*; "This Heat" in *Kansas Quarterly*; "I, Lillian" in *Northward
Journal*; and "A Spinster's Confession Regarding Her Sorrows" in *Milkweed
Chronicle*. The author wishes to thank the editors of these publications for
permission to reprint here. He also wishes to thank James S. Bass and Tom
Redmond for their help with these stories.

Twelve Below Zero has been published with the aid of grants from the Jerome
Foundation, the First Bank System Foundation, the Arts Development Fund of the
United Arts Council, and the McKnight Foundation.

New Rivers Press books are distributed by:

Bookslinger	and	Small Press Distribution
213 E. 4th St.		1784 Shattuck Ave.
St. Paul, MN		Berkeley, CA
55104		94709

Twelve Below Zero has been manufactured in the United States of America for New
Rivers Press, Inc. (C. W. Truesdale, editor/publisher), 1602 Selby Ave., St. Paul, MN
55104 in a first edition of 1000 copies.

For My Mother and Father

TWELVE BELOW ZERO

YOU CAN HEAR ACCORDIONS PLAYING at the End-of-the-Line Cafe. You can curse there, fight and cut (or burn) yourself for sport. You can sip blood soup and hawk and spit among the herring scales on the floor. What I mean is that anything you want there is yours. You can crack walnuts with your teeth or stand on one leg and howl and bark like some creature from Bad River or Isle Royale.

Men are tough at the End-of-the-Line. Some of them have lost toes and fingers to the frost. But no matter, they're still big and strong men. Someone once tried to prove otherwise. He was big, I'll grant, but not so big that we couldn't take care of him. He was a loudmouthed braggart from Blueberry who one night met up with Harry LeCroix. Taking a wallop to the stomach, this loudmouth fell to the floor. That's how hard he'd been hit, or how drunk he was, I forget which. Harry wouldn't let him stand up either. On his hands and knees and by himself, the loudmouth had to make it out the door, had to crawl, not walk, through the spit and herring scales to the door. For who would help him if he couldn't help himself?

Now let me tell you more about the men at the End-of-the-Line Cafe. One of them was Augie Benner, the guy from the sawmill. Another was Thomas Thorsen. They were so unlike each other, so completely and totally different that I still can't understand how they could have done what they did. In addition to Harry LeCroix, the trappers, loggers, and railroad men, there were also Betty Blaine and five or six other women who hung around, among them Bully the Squaw.

And me? I spend nights reading. Mostly, I'm the only one up here who knows how to read and write. I think if the men in the tavern knew, they'd make me crawl like the braggart from Blueberry. But Augie won't tell. He's dead now. And I'd sworn to keep Betty Blaine's secret from others if she wouldn't tell that I study at night. So I guess I'm safe here, and that no one knows I'm writing. Because it's not good to get too smart or to know too much more than the others. Believe me, they'll find out. They'll know if you're getting smart on them, or taking correspondence, or studying under the glow of the oil-lamp with Miss Pesark. They'll mistrust you, and you may even wind up being hurt.

Once in the End-of-the-Line, in fact, a great tragedy occurred to Augie and Tom simply because they were this way — unusual, extraordinary. As the story goes, Mr. Edward Nelson, the Cafe's owner, had hired Tom as a sort of protector of his interests. What a handsome figure the young man made! He was straight and tall and handsome, his eyes always wide, his hair a curly blond. "It looks as if

9

there'll be no spring," was all he said the evening he signed-on. The next he knew, he was protecting Mr. Edward Nelson's property from whatever wildmen fate and the north wind blew his way. Tom was nineteen. Bringing in wood and driving the carriage were all he'd ever done. The rest of the time he spent in the woods hunting. But Nelson convinced the boy to stay and try the bar business awhile. "If you don't, this place will be impossible for me to keep. The business will go under for sure," he said. And so Thomas Thorsen did as he was asked. Had he disobeyed, I'll bet the boss would have promised him more pay. Nelson was fighting for his business-life, for his family's well-being in town.

Tom, on the other hand, ended up fighting for something greater yet, his very life. He began his career against a dairy farmer from Oulu. He ripped half the man's nose away. The dairyman had refused to leave. Some guys couldn't get it through their heads that finally Edward Nelson, the owner, was cleaning the place up, that they were the ones who'd reached the end-of-the-line with *him*. But all the while, this strong, young Thomas Thorsen wanted something better than to breathe the stale air of the End-of-theLine Cafe. In a year, the rough-housing took its toll. He wasn't so quick to laugh, and I didn't hear him much in the tamarack swamps anymore. At the age of twenty, he was turning more serious than before.

I think it was a woman who made the difference. At night when he would leave her, she must have remained in his thoughts, for when he should have been out in the saloon protecting Nelson's interests, the boss would find him in back sitting on a keg of lager, dreaming and singing to himself. If you could see a picture of them, if you can imagine his ever having allowed a wedding photograph of him and Betty Blaine, you would see Tom with his hair parted, his blue eyes sparkling, his face bright and happy, and her at his side, earnest and pretty. But there was never such a wedding photograph. For now comes the wintery part, now the Augie Benner section. If you'll just stay with me while I complete the last part of the triangle of Tom, Betty Blaine and lonesome Augie Benner, I can get on with the story.

He was a sawyer, Augie. The ice, the northerly winds, the frozen earth itself had never inclined him to violence the way it does some men. He'd neither sworn nor lashed out at others that we knew of, certainly not in the End-of-the-Line. Even so, Nelson did not like him much, but for the sake of business would sidle over, inquire of Augie's day, and serve him a sweet drink and a tin of soup and bread. Nelson, looking him directly in the eye, would serve him supper.

Sometimes Augie's skin was pale; sometimes it was so downright unhealthy pale it seemed to me he was ready to die. His hair was like steam, patches of it stuck out from his cap; the weather of his face was gloomy. Occasionally, he pulled his ear, or twitched his eyebrows, or did some other strange thing he probably didn't notice he was doing. But the men did. It was as if the misfortune of the way he smelled, his steam-white hair, and his clothes hanging down were signs of his wasting away, signs of some failing at the core. He'd heard that when children slept, they would complain in their dreams of catching his scent. Or that pretty town girls were afraid of being touched by lonesome Augie's hands. People edged away when he walked down the street, partly because of his looks, partly because of the smell, which I can explain. Up here, you see, someone comes along every now and again who smells as though, well, as though he's worked too long in the canning plants or fisheries south of here. I'm not sure what it is, but even loggers and bartenders find it something unpleasant. We hold our breath when it happens that someone like this arrives in town. Once every few years such a character arrives, and we're suddenly no longer free to breathe God's good air.

But how do you explain Augie? He was no wanderer. He was a citizen living by himself who held steady work in the sawmill. Had he deliberately courted trouble? I wondered. Had be brought on his own? Or was it the sky, the snow, or the wind whistling in the caves of the shore around midnight? I think he was innocent of any wrong doing. For so long now he'd been acting strange. He'd become such a nuisance people shouted at him wherever he went. I guess he was even becoming delighted with himself and the role he'd begun to play. Finally, the smell and the way he acted got so bad we made him wear a bell. Coming down Main Street or walking up behind someone, he was to ring the copper bell hanging about his neck, and that way announce himself so that no one would come too near him. Once we'd made him wear the bell, day after day he faded into his mackinaw so that a person had to examine the shadow between cap, coat and copper bell and whisper, "Augie, is it really *you* so frail and sick?" But every night in spite of his conduct and the condition of his health, he stopped in the Cafe for soup or stew and a hot lemonade. In that way he'd heard of Tom and Betty Blaine. He was way down at the other end, where we made him sit, when he heard of Tom and Betty's good fortune.

It was a blue night, twelve below on the thermometer. He hated the long walk home. Home isn't so good when it's too near the woods. Every spring up here when the daffodils bloom, you hear of the old boatman who'd tried to seek the warmth, light and fellowship of others. You hear of how he fell asleep beneath the ice-glazed trees off Baptism Point; of how, with the snow for a blanket, he closed his eyes and the wind shrove and beat him; and how he slept for a good long time — five months to be exact — before anyone found him, and when they did, strangely enough, dandelion and buttercup were sprouting up through the hood of his mackinaw so that in the light, pleasing breeze, they were rubbing his nose.

Augie hated such long hikes on starless nights when the ghosts of the dead are about. A little later he heard Thomas Thorsen telling Mr. Edward Nelson that he wouldn't go out to fight anymore, that there'd be no more dairymen from Oulu in his future. But Nelson surprised us all.

"Why fight?" Mr. Nelson said. "There's no more reason to. The End-of-the-Line, thanks to you, is all cleaned up. No more fighting here, my boy!" You could see Nelson was overjoyed to run a safe place. "We're going to throw a big dance on the eve of the new moon because of your work, Tom! For you and your sweetie, it's whiskey, bread, and cake!"

Nelson invited us all to come that night on the eve of the moon. He turned to Augie as well. "Say, lonesome Augie," he said, "why not come and help us with the cake? You can help cut and serve it, if you like." But such a request worked salt into his wounds, the sawyer told me later. It was no time for cake, not when it was so cold outside and when he had to get home through the haunted woods.

He'd had pneumonia. How he hated bad weather. He hated his white hair, too, especially when he was only forty-eight years old. I don't suppose it was fair that we should've run from him all those months in the streets. I can't say I liked him. But in this cold I can't stop thinking about it either.

Bully the squaw and another woman came in that night. They laughed at Augie. After that he wouldn't take a refill. He wouldn't look around. Just sat staring straight ahead at the sign that said: STRING CHEESE. EINAR SAYS, "TRY IT, YOU'LL LIKE IT." He'd promised himself about drinking. In this severe country, though, this place where winds set men thinking ill of others, such a thing is hard to avoid, especially after work when there's not much else to do. Augie'd never had a woman as far as we could tell. He had a cabin that was too deep in the woods to wander home to easily.

So there would be dancing and a cake. Augie told me he rather enjoyed a schottische even if he'd never done one. In the Cafe, the guys were laughing. Thomas Thorsen played the accordion and thought of his bride-to-be. Twenty people clapped time. No one remembered Augie's reaching for the whiskey. No one cared — I surely didn't. That night of twelve below zero, lonesome Augie began to hate his condition. And no one, we found, could hate himself like Augie, the sawyer.

Alone at the other end of the bar, he began to do something quite unusual. His steps were way off. No sooner had he set down the bottle than he fell into a dance and jig. He needed no music. Even when the people turned and stared he didn't let up. He was braying and spitting and twisting his body as the bell about his neck began to ring, and his head followed a few beats behind. Jerking his knees and swinging his arms in a sort of rotary fashion, he began to laugh and sing in Swedish.

I was among those urging him on. For a moment I was caught up in the taunting. How easy it was. How simple to be swept up in the crowd. But why should we have picked on one so simple? Because he was Augie, the man with the bad smell and white hair? Because he lived by himself deep in the country and was announced by a copper bell? Or was it the weather and this place, this horrible place? What could have made Nelson and Thorsen strike up their music and let him into their midst? I hate the place and the way they spun him round; the way they grabbed his shirt and pulled him round and made him thrust his head through a bushel basket. When they threw pennies on the dirt floor, he reached for them and the men kicked him with their heavy boots. The bell rang ten times in succession. How the kicks must have hurt! He wore the bushel basket on his head. As he danced, the spit flew from his mouth. Later, he told me he'd never danced; later, he asked me, why in his joy was he not any happier? The hair flapping up and down on the side of his head, the bell ringing, I remember how he started to tire, how he must have wondered as he danced why he'd ever come this far north in the first place, why he'd ever left Trempeleau. With everyone laughing he asked aloud what he was doing. It was so funny. His arms high, his head bobbing out of time, the bushel basket falling back and forth, the bell tolling requiem, he saw someone coming toward him, reaching out to him. To dance a schottische? To waltz him from the old, dark north? Lowering the basket to dance with Thorsen, he hugged the boy gently to him and kissed him full on the mouth for the longest time....

After this, there are no photographs of Thomas Thorsen, neither with an accordion, nor with the children he would go on to raise. He may never have had another photo taken for all we know. He also threw all mirrors out of his house. He didn't want to see his face again. He had fallen to the floor after returning Augie's kiss, and the sawyer hurried home through the woods.

He returned the next day looking for the boy. But, ashamed of what he'd done in the End-of-the-Line, Thomas was out seeking another job, though avoiding the sawmill where lonesome Augie worked. Augie, too, was fearful. Only at odd times would he sneak into the backroom of the Cafe. At least once every twenty-four hours, he came round, if only for a minute, to ask Mr. Edward Nelson about the meaning of love and what he, Augie, had felt for the boy that night of the new moon. Night after night, no matter the wind or the snow or the howling of beasts, he came. Nelson told him nothing, however. For some things defy explaining. The rest of the time the sawyer stayed in his cabin.

This is the part I like the least in Augie Benner's history; how sunrise came and noons and nightfalls and how for his troubles he saw the river freezing deep and the wolves deriding the moon outside his cabin door. Still, he came round looking for Tom. He was like the old boatman needing to talk to someone, or to just plain kiss someone. Neither I, nor Nelson, nor Harry LeCroix could tell him anything. For too often, I've found, things have hidden meanings. A person accepts this fact and goes on about the day's business, careful in the cold weather to protect himself.

"Tell me, please, where's Tom?" he'd ask. And Nelson would answer him, "I can't tell you. I don't know where he is these days or why he'd kiss *you*." Then Nelson would close the door at the End-of-the Line Cafe. What customers were left shuffled around and coughed before slipping past him on the way home. But Nelson's answer was never enough for Augie. Nelson told him he didn't know because he didn't, not really. I didn't either. Which is what I'm trying to under-stand — how so much is inexplicable about a man's conduct sometimes. You think you can examine and explain it. But in the process, and in spite of what you tell yourself you've found, you still know you've come up empty-handed. It's like the wind blowing twigs over the snow; the patterns they make are hard to decipher.

I am an historian who observes the place he lives in. I've suffered through its regional and community tragedies. A man's crazy coming up here if he has no reason to. After the kiss, Augie lived at the mercy of another person. Surrounded by lakes, one as deep as the next, he and the rest of us were trapped. But Augie, surely, would never get out, not with someone stalking him. He was suddenly more a victim than he'd ever been. When he was out, someone broke into his cabin, throwing a dog's carcass on the bed which became spattered with blood. They tormented his nights, so that he came to believe in spirits. I guess he was truly giving up, drying out for the northerly winds to scatter his ashes more easily.

Then the shots started. It was as if lakes, forest and sky conspired against the little, white-haired man with the bell. He couldn't tell where they were coming from. It was if something bred in the mystery of darkness and the heart had made this north country frantic — and him so miserable for love. That's what started happening; there was something tragic abroad in the night shooting at the doors and windows of his cabin. Was it the bleak northern place itself revolting against his expression of love?

He wore rags, Augie did, lonesome Augie. And the bell still clanged about his neck. Sometimes I thought it would strangle him. Then there were moments when he had to hide in the woods, hands over his ears, to avoid what they were saying in town. But their words seemed to echo in the trees, and they wouldn't be silent for a long time. The words came with the wind; the snow brought them.

It was Betty Blaine who came to me finally. Not Mr. Edward Nelson, the saloon-keeper, not the Thorsen family, or someone else. But Betty Blaine. History marked her husband as the man who was kissed by Augie (and who kissed him in return). This was a fact she could not easily live with. I forgot to say they had been married true enough in spite of Augie's kiss. What rankled Betty Blaine Thorsen now was the wasting of Tom's life. "Does he really like lonesome Augie?" people were asking in whispers. Now it was Betty who was aging like Augie. No older than her husband, nevertheless, her eyes became sunken and dark and wrinkles appeared in her brow. She blushed at fewer things. Until one night she sought me like a charm. Augie Benner used to do that, too. It wasn't for advice that Betty sought me, but for support in what she planned to do.

Now I have to tell the story alone. There's no more Augie. The terrorizing of this man had been going on for months. She said nothing about that, nor even why she'd come to a man she hardly knew. Perhaps she thought I would tell her something I'd learned in books, something about putting aside knife and rifle. I don't know my own mind, my own *self* very well. So how could I tell her what was right to do? But I listened to her like a damned fool and was cursed. Before, I was innocent. I didn't know her story and was free of the guilt of knowing. But now, having listened, I knew. I had knowledge. "Do you know how I have been hurt because of that sawyer's act ... actions?" she asked me.

She came again another morning. There was enough light to see through the woods. My windows were frozen over but the wind stopped blowing and I could see her outline. She pounded on the door and pushed it open. She walked to the fire and said a few things.

She came a third time, too, then a fourth. She came tapping on the windows, and I saw ice dangling from her coat and snow on her brow and frost beneath her nails when she removed her heavy gloves....

Then a fifth time. It was early morning and she said how she'd pierced the sawyer's body; how he'd bled; how he'd bled and crawled and said something terrible about love; how he kept repeating the terrible things to her; and how she'd tracked him for as far as he could go. "You can find the trail. There's no sawyer. He's a red scar on the face of the earth now," she said, "and you can go and find the trail and the bell yourself."

After that she left. "I don't need your fire now," she said. I blocked my ears too late from the sound of her voice and what she was telling me. Who am I to tell? I am no longer innocent of knowing. I know too much; more than the others except Betty, and she doesn't care about her knowledge so she's free of its burden. That's how knowing works. It's a burden unless you don't care. I have read too much with Miss Pesark not to care. I know about lonesome Augie what no one else does — how he died in the cold.

Following the red path, I found the place where Augie and Tom's wife had so recently disturbed the peace. A crust of blood and ice had formed around him. To get to the bell, I removed his hat. His hair blew in the wind, and I covered him with snow and let him sleep. Except for in the west, the sky was clear, the surface snow whipping around. If you looked once, the sun was out. If you looked again, it was behind the snow. It was an odd thing the way that happened. I've seen it snow hard for six days, but what's the difference without a wind? That day there was a wind. It was difficult finding my way back, the bell about my neck.

Thomas Thorsen's working again, I've found. Betty's resting at home these days expecting another child. Free to go to other interests, they are absolved, avenged, well-rested. They (or *she* anyway) has done what she set out to do, avenged herself and Thomas Thorsen. So everyone's working or resting now and happy around here. But I? I am a party to it. I have to tell the story of the killing of Augie Benner or go mad in the silence of my room. As far as Betty and the others, they're done with it. But I'm left thinking of the boatman. And what if I should meet bloody Augie this night on the pathway in to town without having told his story yet? And what if he should touch me with that fearsome touch? He tried to tell someone what he felt and look where it got him. I don't want to end up speechless within sight of town and with dandelion and buttercup in my hair next summer. Or to be blown about in strange ways like the twigs on the snow. Or hugged by someone known to be an outsider. But what then? Why, I wonder, why should I, who for his own protection must pretend he can't even read and write, be burdened with this secret and be the curst of God? I can't stop thinking that it's unfair to me that I should have to wear the bell meant for another. I am tired now. I pace my room, stare at the fireplace, and think about what I wish I didn't know — things about life, about Betty and about Augie Benner and the meaning of love. Sometimes I have to go away fast to where the snow sifts through pines, barely settling on the fur of the whitetail; to where the wind can't get at me if I hide my head deep in my hands to muffle the sounds of what they're saying about me in town. Tonight the forest is too loud for that, though. Practically every night lately there have been such rumors howling in the woods that I haven't been going out much.

THE CHILDREN OF STRANGERS

Ralph and Josephine Slipkowski live on Raspberry Avenue in a two bedroom bungalow which is not raspberry-colored but green with white trim. They have a brass doorknob and an American eagle door knocker, which nobody uses. Next to the door in summer a planter full of petunias cheers things up, glads on the side, marigolds out back. A beautiful sugar maple grows in their yard in Superior, Wisconsin, a railroad and port city whose motto "Superior —Where Rail Meets Sail" was coined during a Chamber of Commerce meeting at the Androy Hotel on Tower Avenue. When it doesn't rain for a time Ralph Skipkowski trims and waters his lawn. With knife and spade, he edges a border along the sidewalk so no weeds can grow. When Josephine needs support he's there, especially of late when she's begun doubting things. Most people wouldn't believe anyone living in a well-kept house, whose appearance its owners take pride in preserving, would be distraught. Most people wouldn't think so, since houses like this should project their owner's stability and be signatures of the well-kept existence. Josie and Ralph's is a modern, two bedroom bungalow, but Josie Slipkowski's problems aren't modern.

When Josie and Ralph examine themselves in the living room mirror, they see two people in decline. Ralph's been spending a lot of time in rooms with mirrors. This night Josephine arranges her hair, her husband his tie. Actually only Josie understands what's occurring around her. She sees no very good future for herself, not since the doubting began. Neither family nor *self* cause her to doubt this way. But something does. She thinks of it as, even calls it "the verge of time," though never in front of Ralph. For Ralph just doesn't see what's going on, Josie thinks. He's missing the sign for The End when it stands right there before him in the mirror or just outside on the street. Ralph has been kind and thoughtful their entire married life. So have the kids. But he just doesn't see what's happening. He has nothing to fear; he can't read the sign in the mirror.

"You can tell expensive ones, really good mirrors, by placing a fingertip to the glass," he says. "There'll be an eighth inch, maybe more, reflected from where your fingertip touches to where the other begins. Cheap mirrors don't reflect so deeply as expensive ones. Expensive mirrors express a person better."

The oak dresser with Ralph and Josie's most expensive mirror stands in a house on an elm-lined street of houses which were kept up once, but now grow steadily shabbier. The houses in Superior deteriorate when they aren't looked after, when they aren't painted, when little things go wrong. They've gotten so because people are out of work. The cold, rainy, foggy weather of spring and summer only makes matters worse for the people and their houses, but not Ralph Slipkowski's house, for even in retirement, he's a tireless, meticulous worker, especially in a room with mirrors around. The mirror on the oak dresser stands like a heart at the center of his house.

Four nuns reside a few miles from Ralph and Josie's. *Skǫła Wojciecha* means "Albert, or Adalbert School." The pupils there have names like Maretski, Mizinski, Symzyk, Lalko, and Urbaniak. They are more sober and industrious today than their parents were in school, for a strange thing has happened. Stanislaus Wysinski, the Slipkowski's neighbor, has taken his boy to the window, pointed to section hands laying track on the Great Northern, and said, "You straighten out in school, son, or when you're old, you'll be hiding sand under the ties!" and Josef Stasiak, in an effort to get his grandson back in school, told the boy, who'd quit to work on the coal docks, "*Chciał es teraz ma'sz*. You wanted it, now you have it." Ralph Slipkowski was like that with his own sons. Ralph's life, Josie will tell you, hasn't been easy. He's wished for better, maybe a three-or-four chair barber shop. He's wanted the best for the boys. But there for a time when they wouldn't study, he'd had to lay down the law. "This is *my* shop. As long as you're in *my* shop," he'd call it, "you'll do as *I* say."

"So, Ralph," Josephine says, "if life isn't easy for the sisters — one of them has to do the laundry, cooking, and cleaning — they at least have a job. Sister Bronislaw is the last of the old ones. Think of her years here!"

Ralph comes into the living room. In a vain effort to forestall her own decline, Josie primps before the mirror. "Is this tie on straight?" Ralph asks.

"Those kids in the neighborhood drive the nuns crazy ... Yes, it is, Ralph ... it's straight ... Right back to the Motherhouse go the sisters, one after another. But lately it seems worse."

Ralph rubs Butch Wax in his hair. After twenty-eight years, he still uses it. He still goes to Mass after twenty-eight years of marriage too, but irregularly. Ralph and Josie had talked and talked before he let the boys attend St. Adalbert's School when they were of age. "It's my duty to give them a Catholic education," Josie had argued. "Why don't you feel the same?"

"The public schools are fine," Ralph had said, "but if your heart's set on it, then OK."

The boys are out of school now and gone, and the old-timers leaving, thinks Josie. *Their houses become defiled.* She thinks of how the city moves indigent families into vacant houses near the Slipkowski's when public housing near the Fraser Shipyards is full. It's nothing intentional, she knows, nothing against her and Ralph, but at the moment most of the vacant houses are near theirs. Some of the Polish people have died, others have gone away in search of work. The city purchases their houses for well below market value, and in rush the newcomers. Now the children of strangers break glass on the sidewalks, roar down the alleys on motorcycles, and let their dogs run loose in the streets. These people who put up grease racks in the yard, Josephine has wondered, where do they come from

— out near Iron River or Brule? Her husband glances once more in the mirror, glances fearlessly at himself in the expensive mirror on his grandmother's dresser.

Josephine straightens her collar, sprays a reluctant curl with VO 5. Ralph Slipkowski still putters around the room. The boys are gone, Josie thinks, I'm getting older. Was it so easy raising two children, keeping house, and staying out of debt when business was off or Ralph sick? she wonders. She recalls the struggle, like the time Ralph went to a two-chair shop in a new place and found out that his partner was a philanderer. Ralph's customers already knew about it. Business fell off until Ralph returned to working alone.

For the past few months, even a year now, the sisters have been on Josie's mind the way mirrors have been on Ralph's. The nuns live in the neighborhood with newcomers who can't get into shipyard housing. Sister Stella, Sister Cecilia, and Sister Appolonia have come and gone. Their coifs were made of hard, white, starched cloth. Their wimples thrust sharply out from the neck. Their lacquered beads swung at their sides as they walked. But Sister Bronislaw has three new sisters to keep her company. The good sisters of *Skoł a Wojciecha* care lovingly for Father Nowak's vestments, order votive candles, sweep the sacristy, lead the choir, train altar boys, teach classes, supervise, pray. Before lunch they've prayed several hours.

But despite prayer and supplication, they are declining, Josephine thinks. Even sensitive eighth-graders will observe the nuns growing old, their own parents losing the mother tongue, the neighborhood, well ... failing. In the early years of this school, Sister Bronislaw's pupils believed in something. In the year the cornerstone was set, 1916, they were sensitive to the blood heritage which she was part of. When she shook her students they learned fear and admiration. The trainer of wayward Polish youth, Sister Bronislaw instructed them — she trained us, *me*, Josie thinks — to work diligently at home and school, honor the Polish flag, and grow up in the faith. Now the neighborhood's gone to hell with people of different faith, or of no faith at all. "People without a heritage who draw public assistance have overtaken us, Ralph," she says to her husband, Mr. Slipkowski.

He's looking in the bedroom mirror now. Fearing nothing, he moves from mirror to mirror, room to room, good mirrors, bad mirrors. In the expensive mirror on his grandmother's dresser, the one in the bedroom, he can see himself reflected better. In fact, it's such a good mirror that he can almost see the past in it. His own past has never troubled him much, not this barber, this sole owner and proprietor of a one-chair shop at Belknap and Ogden in Superior.

"Ralph Slipkowski!" she calls.

He appears with a flourish. "Yes, I'm ready," he says. His hair is gray. It stands up with Butch Wax. The gray matches his tweed jacket. "It begins at 7:30, doesn't it?" he asks. His face beams with good will. "Let's say goodbye to the old girl." He jiggles the car keys. He helps Josephine with her coat. It is early winter in Josie Slipkowski's soul. What's coming will be worse yet, she thinks. She doubts her ability to survive it. Even extinction might be better than doubting, she thinks.

"We've done OK, Ralph, haven't we?"

In the car she thinks of Sister Bronislaw. For a moment she doesn't know whom she's talking to, like the good sister is there with them.

"*Jak szybko mija chwile*," Josie says aloud. "How quickly flies every moment."

She hears Ralph's chuckle.

"What was that?" he asks.

"I was dreaming of sister. Are you listening, Ralph? It's OK if you don't."

I understand you, Ralph, my dear. He drives on, content with himself. *You've done much good for the nuns and Father*, Josie thinks. *Our sons are grown and gone away. And if you don't listen to me all the time now what does it matter? For twenty-eight years you've listened carefully. It's just that I don't know what our future holds. We're losing. I'm certain the strength of our family, our generation, is slipping away. Our boys, Al and Terry, won't have the strength the sisters brought with them from the old country. We are in decline, Ralph Slipkowski, and I am afraid.*

Ralph checks the rear view mirror. He signals, turns up 5th Street. He goes by Van Damme's Plumbing, the East End Library.

You're a harmless, good man whose shortcomings are modest ones. You, Al and Terry never shared the sense of history with me. Sometimes I fear for myself. It was an odd, holy house I grew up in. Blessed candles were stuck away in drawers and Holy Water in different rooms. Black crepe on the door signalled death. If we dropped bread, Grandma made us kiss it. History haunts me. You and the boys don't know how bad. Now we must look over our shoulders and lock our doors when we leave the house.

Humming, Ralph drives effortlessly. He passes the Northern Block. He turns a block down at the intersection by the drugstore and the bank.

Looking out the window, Josephine sees Mrs. Pawlokoski and Mrs. Fronckiewicz, two Polish ladies, walking arm in arm. They are going the same way as the Slipkowskis. They wave. Ralph pulls onto 4th Street.

"Those old people...." he says.

But Josephine Slipkowski does not dismiss them so readily, for in the dread winter hour — December, January, February, March, part of April — Mrs. Cieslicki, Mrs. Kiszewski, Mr. Pomerinski, Mr. Tomazeski, Sister Bronislaw are all here worshipping in the church of Polish immigrants. They come to Mass then and every other day. When the weather turns bad the sisters and elderly parishioners pray as though it were any other season of the year. Nothing sways their purpose. Why do old, weary legs fight the way here? Why do weary spirits arise in winter to walk to a cold church where sometimes a visiting priest celebrates Mass? The old people come for the visiting priest's Mass at six, mornings, then stay for Father's at eight. Over the years Josie Slipkowski has justified her faith this way, justified her own faith through the faith of others.

She has come to realize that out of all the old people, including her own grandma *Babusha*, out of all the immigrants from Poznan and Szczecin, Warsaw and Bialystok, at least one must have known more than simple, blind faith to come each morning in prayer. This person — the peasant from Lodz, the baker from Katowice, the noble from Ziolona Gora — must have had assurance, here or in the old country, that getting out of bed was going to be worth it. What Polish immigrants have over the newcomers is continuity, thinks Josie, a faith that has lasted long and travelled far.

Skoł a Wojciecha stands at 3rd Street and 22nd Avenue. From there you can look out and see King Midas Flour, the oil dock, Hog Island and Minnesota Point. Father rings the church bell this night. Ralph pulls up before Mrs. Konchack's garage. She comes out, waving her red *babushka*. "It's OK," she says. "*To dobrze*," and Ralph and Josie join other parishioners. Downstairs you can smell coffee and flowers, cigarette smoke and baked goods. You can hear the roar of parish voices punctuated by laughter and song. Mr. Adam Burbul, Mr. and Mrs. Tomazeski, Augie and Louie Fronckiewicz and their mother and sisters, good, patient Helen Stromko from the dime store, the Nicoskis, Johanna Havanac, Mrs. Cieslicki, Mrs. Podgorak — two hundred have assembled on a Thursday evening. How Josephine Slipkowski wishes Al and Terry, who went here eight years and played basketball in this hall, could see it, and her grandmother and grandfather, *Babusha* and *Jadusz*, who are dead.

Anthony Coda, a classmate from 1934, a red-and-white carnation in his lapel, stands by the door with Matthew Burbul. Ralph finds Josephine a chair. Father Nowak appears soon after the church bell has stopped. On stage sits Sister Bronislaw. The parishioners sing "*Jeszcze Polska Nie Zgineł a*."

How we're losing, thinks Josephine Slipkowski. *Except for their years at Skoł a Wojciecha, what will distinguish the young who change their names and move away? Beyond St. Adalbert's, what remains? Beyond Sister Bronislaw....?*

Josephine recalls her mother telling her how, in the old times, Sister Bronislaw went door to door to houses under quarantine in the neighborhood. A purple card on the door meant typhoid, red meant scarlet fever. They were placed there by the Health Department. Sister Bronislaw would inquire, "Do you need some food, *Pani* Zimski? Driftwood ... forest wood?" No, she was not weak, Josie thinks.

The gym's beige-and-green paint has faded and chipped; the hardwood floor, though waxed recently, is warped beyond repair. Steam pipes run along the walls. The Rosary Society has decorated them with red-and-white bunting. All the old parishioners are here.

"The old Polish people won't be with us much longer," Josephine says to Ralph. Sister herself has been here half-a-century, Josie thinks. Maybe not a week or month and we'll read in the news that all of them have finally gone away.

Some of the old ones speak no English. Those who do sing "Joining Poland's sons and daughters, we'll be Poles forever" before Father clears his throat. Except for his voice, the hall is quiet.

"Tonight is an honor," he says. "We're here to give you this tribute, Sister Bronislaw."

Settling her hands in her lap, sister leans forward. She gazes at Father and down at the parishioners in the gym. She holds the gift now, a little unsteadily — a red box with a white bow around it; a scapular, thinks Josie Slipkowski, a book of the Lives of the Saints wrapped in the colors of Poland. Sister Bronislaw clasps it to her as she looks out at the walls she has known so long and at the people: a Polish priest, a former novitiate, a grocer and a newsman, a teacher and a banker and a switchman on the Great Northern. Unsure of what to do, sister clutches the gift to the crucifix hanging from a gold chain around her neck. The parishioners thanks go with the gift. They stand up to applaud her.

"*Co to?*" she says with a quizzical look. "This? What's this?"

Father Nowak then reads a letter of congratulations and good wishes from the Bishop. Later, as others praise Sister Bronislaw, Sister Digna plays "God, Who Held Poland" on the piano. The old hall rings with haunted melodies that hurt a person with their sadness, the unforgotten music of the past. How can you describe the music? Chopin ... Paderewski ... It is something romantic and sensitive.

The outsiders arrive the way they've been coming for centuries. Just as Sister Bronislaw and the others sing "*Jeszcze Polska*" again, they hear the slow, airy settling of the door, followed by footsteps. Having seen lights, no doubt the newcomers figured on shooting baskets in the gymnasium. The old Polish people, as they prepare to be invaded, hear them chattering, snapping their gum, bouncing the ball. Except for an occasional cough and some scraping of chairs the hall is quiet. Even Father Nowak with the Bishop's letter tucked away in his jacket and Sister Bronislaw in her chair on the stage turn their eyes to the entrance at the bottom of the stairs, anticipating the noise, the violent entry into their lives.

The two defiant boys in torn jackets walk in as though it is their right. The children of strangers, they have invaded the neighborhood and now the school. They come and go freely. As the young ones roam the alleys, their older brothers accost the meek and humble.

When they see the old Polish people the two boys stop. Hunched over, chewing their gum, they stare at the face of Poland, whose age and civility mean nothing to them. One boy is pasty looking. Dark circles ring his eyes. The other, having tried growing a moustache, has succeeded in raising a few stringy hairs on the upper lip. The two boys, not over thirteen or fourteen, waver there. They do not attend this school. Perhaps they've never been in its gym. Or perhaps, having found Mr. and Mrs. Novozinski, Albert Roubal, the Ste ankos, and two hundred others, the boys have discovered Mrs. Josephine Slipkowski's "verge of time" and can't break free again to darkness and the night, not yet. For in finding the old people, they have found the past. It catches their imagination.

22

On the western front in 1939, Polish horse soldiers, their drawn swords raised and gleaming, charged German armored tanks. Defiantly, quixotically, soldiers from another century charged into the mechanical age and disappeared in the smoke. At the same time in Poland, young airmen practiced maneuvers in glider planes. When Poland was finally lost to the enemy, the Polish State Radio broadcast a polonaise and fell silent. The radio went off the air with something for dreamers.

Now in the gymnasium of the Polish school, it is as if, through some stroke of fate, two intruders have discovered a forest clearing from which to observe horse soldiers gearing for the last, violent, fatal charge. In their one brief moment, the two witness for the first time their neighbors' nobility. It is evident in how the old people have turned out to honor the nun, how they've kept up their traditions and faith. While it has taken Josephine some months of constant doubting to observe, then accept the newcomers' disregard for others, these children of strangers have taken only a minute to learn about centuries of struggle, and grow bored. Wearying of the moment, the boys no longer appear to care what has been discovered this night. You could give them Sobieski charging the Turks, thinks Josie, Dobrowski praying in his tent for a safe return home, the Black Madonna pierced in the side and crying, Unrug at the Battle of Hel. You could throw in Thaddeus Kosciusko freeing Warsaw from the Russians in the Spring of 1794, and the two intruders wouldn't care. These things resonate in the air about them. They lie in the mirrors in the Polish homes and in the wrinkles of the old faces and in the eyes and deep within the memory.

But the intruders have never known doubt. They bounce the ball, then spy the table with the food and cake for Sister Bronislaw. One of the boys puts up a shot. The basketball, falling through, rips the paper decoration hanging from the net. It is a long, hopeless, ugly moment as they saunter to the table which is laden with sweetbreads, hot dishes, hams, cheese, pickles, the large white cake. Let them eat their fill, thinks Josephine Slipkowski. Let them fill up, be done with us, leave us. As long as the old ones are alive, she thinks, somewhere, always, a polonaise will be playing.

The one who sees differently now is her husband Ralph. All his life he has looked on the bright side of things and left other people alone. But tonight in the gym, the intruders have seen him and walked right past him. They did not look at but *through* him with their smirking faces as though he counted for nothing at all on this earth. That's when he had a sort of vision of things. It is not Josie but Ralph Slipkowski whose thinking about mirrors changes. More and more in the coming days, he sees in this vision, riots will be tearing cities apart and presidents and dignitaries will be seized and put upon. It is not Josie's, but Ralph's thinking that's changed. And now, of all things, he's suddenly becoming frightened of looking in mirrors.

THE WOMAN WHO ATE CAT FOOD

ONCE, BEFORE SHE WENT TO HELL, Margaret Markham had a social encounter. In view of her preoccupation with telephones, you could say this social encounter was with "the man on the other end." The two of them dined out a lot, generally using the "Carriage Trade Plan" she'd sold him over the telephone, for she was a telephone solicitor who worked out of a room in her apartment and one day made a sale which, well, blossomed into a romance. The Carriage Trade Plan entitles you, for a $20.50 yearly investment, to purchase a meal and receive another free at certain less-distinguished, but nevertheless good, New Orleans restaurants. Her telephone lead, the man whom she contacted and with whom she eventually fell in love, used his card all over the city and soon the shrimp creole and crawfish étoufée began to show around his waist.

"Margaret," he said the last Wednesday of their "friendship." He'd come with ashes on his forehead. "Margaret, the kids, Greta, and I ... we're leaving. Business has called me away up north, dear."

With all the sweet potato pecan pie and the beignets at the Cafe du Monde, he'd gained probably forty pounds. He was no longer the man Margaret encountered over the telephone some months before. She watched him leave for good one rainy Saturday. From a cafe window, she saw the difficult time he had getting into his car. The months of very passionate suppers had marked him, blown him up so that he could have used a fast during Lenten season when the devout deny themselves pleasures. A fast, too, would have gone well with the ashes on his forehead. In a phone booth on Rue Royale, Margaret Markham scribbled down numbers off of a wall. Since any number would do, she called 338-9185 and struck up a conversation with a Daniel Morgan who soon after lodged a complaint with South Central Bell. "Intentional annoyance by use of the phone ... The maximum penalty for violation is ... " they warned her.

After this, except for telephone contacts she made from her room, it was as if Margaret Markham no longer existed. She would sit in the dim, cold room ruminating on possible telephone talks she could have with the man in Apt. 24 next door. It was simple: if he would call just once, if he would call and say something hopeful, it would mean the way out of failure through, what? friendship? love? She waited for his call. She grew weak with waiting, brittle in the knees waiting for the call from Apt. 24. If she did go out, she took the back way. For a time you'd think she was on holiday. Then someone, perhaps the man next door in Apt. 24, would spot her locking her door and hurrying Lord knows where — to the wharf by the Jax Brewery, to the ferry for Algiers.

The man next door, who is a writer of petty, mean-spirited reviews and obscure articles, would say someone has taken poetic license with him. "I didn't deny her as often as you'd think," he'd say in his defense to Fred and Marta, relatives of the deceased who'd flown in directly after Margaret's tragedy. By then it didn't matter. As they were winging their way in from Dallas, Margaret herself was well on her way somewhere else after a not-too-happy life telephoning others about — Marta would say this rather snidely — about "siding on their houses, warranties on their appliances, insurance on their lov—, on their lives. Look, I almost said *loves* a minute ago, Fred! I almost said 'Insurance on their loves.!' "

"That's funny," Fred says. They are standing in the hallway outside her apartment, making the aquaintance of the man next door. Fred has barely had time to unpack his bags at a nearby hotel and take a look around the French Quarter before coming over. He strokes the cat, Belvedere, who has just returned from chasing Margaret Markham's ghost through the city's streets and alleys. The police who discovered Margaret Markham said that when they opened the window of her apartment, the cat leapt out, landing on its paws, and took off down Tchoupitoulas Street after her spirit. "It's sure frightening to think so," they'd said.

"Without this little rascal to keep her sane," Fred says, now holding the cat in his arms, "she might have gotten a touch-tone, a black, touch-tone telephone instead of the dial-type she had, or she might have had the phone disconnected entirely."

"So instead she went and disconnected herself," says Marta. "To think my sister—"

"I know one thing," says the man next door. He is a university teacher, not even full-time and not at Tulane or the University of New Orleans, but at one of the city's smaller schools. "I know it was hard getting hold of her for anything. I bumped into her once, one of those days she'd gone out. By the way, may I call you Fred and Marta?"

They are getting more comfortable with one another, more cheerful.

"Please," says Fred. "Why all the formality in the first place?"

"As I said, I bumped into her once," the man next door in Apt. 24 says. "She was winded from climbing those stairs. I looked in on her and found her making phone calls. '3409 is busy,' she'd say and look at me. '7041, Hello? Mr. Armstead?' She'd turn and say, 'He hung up!' Then she'd dial again. '5445? Mr. Schuster?' She was a telephone solicitor in the worst way, I guess, totally committed to telephone communication."

"That's my sister," Marta replies.

"One time I found her eating from a can of Belvedere's food too, Fred. You know, the only calls she ever got were from teenagers, cranks. 'Do you have Prince Albert in the can?' they'd ask. She'd hear them laughing, then that...click and the line goes dead. They'd hang up on her. She'd be alone giggling. One night she told me this and a lot of other things I'd asked her about."

"Maybe that's when she thought of having it disconnected," Fred says, "when she got the crank calls."

"I don't know. Maybe. She found out who *I* was from my mailbox."

"This is a good cat," Fred says. "You wonder what-all he's witnessed."

"Yes, you do wonder what that cat has seen," agrees the man next door. "All I know is she'd make plenty of phone calls, then, exhausted, she'd spoon out her anxieties, you might say, with Bel's Moist Meals and Junior Friskies. She had secrets galore."

"She was always that way," Marta says.

"She padded her shoes with paper towels when her shoes got too big for her," says the neighbor. He is a writer of petty, mean-spirited reviews and obscure articles. "That's one thing she told me. Do you remember when she was nineteen, Marta? When she lost her boyfriend? He had to go in early, she told me. No sooner had she left him than two other girls came by and went in the house. She told me how she stood there out of sight hugging the rotting barn, watching for him. Anyway what kind of name is Marta?"

"Scandinavian. We moved down from Nebraska."

"Do you remember the time her boyfriend did that to her?"

"I remember," says Marta. "She came home laughing. 'Ma,' she said, 'I lost. I saw two girls just now come by to get my boyfriend which means his mother knew too, so I was doubly deceived."

"Were they a Catholic family?" our mother asked. "She was always careful to see that they were, wasn't she, Fred? My grandfather had converted, and she wanted us to go out with Catholic boys."

"Isn't it kind of cold for Fat Tuesday?" asks Fred

The man next door says that it is. "Fred and Marta, you should have been here a week ago. It was warm, hot even," he exudes.

"At the age of forty-three with her hair the color of ash she must have waited for you, for *us*, to call her," Marta is saying. "Don't you think?"

"Listen!" says Fred. He cups his ear and turns in the direction of the French Quarter. "You can hear Mardi Gras."

"You know, my sister always tended to colors like dust and ash and the brown of dead berries. She knew how to celebrate Lent, too."

"I'd say so," says the neighbor, "a very passionate celebrant, your sister. For her there was no resurrection, just fast and abstain day after day. 'Hello,' she'd say, 'Mr. Mitchell, 879-6453? It's Margaret Markham for Delta Aluminum. I wonder if we couldn't have a brief talk about your siding, which our company noticed —'"

"'Thanks, no!'" he'd tell her.

"'Mr. Reginald Fortier? I've called to see if we couldn't talk insurance —'"

"'No, thanks.'"

"I guess that's what her life should amount to," says Fred, "an empty, white page to go along with the black touch-tone she always wanted. She was a blank."

"Then she met you," Marta says to the neighbor. "What did you do to her?"

"Not a thing. I came in once after rapping on the door and getting no answer. I found her sitting with an empty glass to her ear. She was holding it in the direction of my apartment. She'd been listening to the wall, trying to hear me. When she saw me she looked up and said, 'Do you know what you find when you dial yourself on the telephone? — that on the other end, you yourself are busy.' That's all! That's what she said. All your sister had in the final analysis was a busy signal telling her her line was engaged. All she had was the outside world by telephone and my capricious humor next door. Heh, heh," he chuckles to himself, forgiving his shortcomings which, after all, are modest ones, he feels.

"What I can't figure out," says Fred, "is how anyone could be *that* lonely. Now take Marta and me, sure we get lonesome sometimes, but not so bad that we'd — Why was she caught here like this? I guess she was just weary of people not talking, or being rude, or filing complaints. This all seems kind of ridiculous now."

"To me, too. It's a little late now to be of much help. Except maybe to you, Marta," says the man next door.

"Thank you. I appreciate this, your sympathy. She had a confused life, but I never expected it was this bad."

The neighbor looks up and down the hall. It is bleak and quiet. The three of them huddle under the light.

"Maybe I shouldn't tell you this, but I was in there, in her place, one of her last nights when she made some calls for, I guess it was Eastside Awnings. A guy named Kruk answered. I guess he wept, then swore at her. Do you know what she said? 'Mr. Kruk, talk to me, please. I want to hear you. No don't hang up tonight. It's too close to Ash Wednesday.' This guy Kruk told her his wife Myrna was in a rest home and his son Jerry in the Navy over in Rota. He must have been off his rocker. He started yelling over the telephone. I could even hear him from where I stood. 'Railroad has laid me off.... Twenty-nine years I go day and night. What do I need your awnings? Damn them to hell? All awnings! Goddamn them ...all of them to everlasting hell! So why do I deserve this? The Church can go to hell ... and goddamn hell. Ralph, my brother, he's got bone cancer. You tell me it's fair now!'"

"This is what I think," Marta says. "She'd just been alone too long to live with and couldn't go on. She loved all these people she called. In her strange way she always loved the suffering, guys like Mr. Kruk. Maybe even you for ever letting her speak to you," she says to the neighbor. "But she'd gone this way too long. She probably didn't know how she spent her time anymore. If I know my sister, she probably even talked to herself in mirrors."

"She was the sole companion of the self," the neighbor adds.

"She was a human being who never loved much and, you tell me now, she even succeeded in eating cat food. Cheated, she went away. My poor sister Margaret."

"She'd put down the telephone, I'll bet," Fred says. "The busy signal was in her ears. It was getting very serious. Yes, that's what happened."

"Why didn't we help her and come over from Dallas, Fred? Why didn't we make her more than a footnote in our lives? She must have felt so helpless holding the telephone receiver to her head as though it were a ... gun, a clock, a portable radio and she was here waiting for the forecast."

"I bet she put Belvedere here in the closet. Did she do that, Bel, did she?" Fred asks. "Then she closed the door, I'll bet. She must have written the letters to us from the kitchen. Putting them in envelopes, she'd leave them in the mailbox for the postman."

"Which meant she went downstairs one last time," says the neighbor.

"Yes," says Fred, "that's how we all got the news — her letters. Then she probably looked in on the cat, maybe freshened its water before returning to her place by the stove where she could sit reviewing her phone bills. What do you think? Was that how it was?"

"I just know what the police and fire people said, that the cat jumped out when they opened the closet door and bedroom window," replies the neighbor.

"We know this much," Marta says. "It chased her spirit."

"Where have you been, Bel?" asks the neighbor. "Which way did Margaret go, up or down?"

"Do you suppose she's in heaven? It's too horrible to think otherwise," says Marta.

"Did I tell you I'm writing a story? I've come to see through all this that no one should neglect suffering. I've found that much out anyway, and I am genuinely sorry about your sister." The man next door takes Marta's hand for the moment, shaking it gently. "It's tragic," he says. "The day of her death she mailed something to me. It came in a white envelope with the smell of gas still clinging to it. It's the enigma of your sister Margaret. She didn't hardly write anything. It arrived two days later the best I can figure it. It took two whole days to go what? Five feet? Isn't it something what the postal service gets away with? All she had to do was walk over and open my door, thus saving stamps. But here comes a letter instead. In the middle of a legal-sized sheet she wrote five lousy words, 'I, suffering, am done for.' Why did she mail them? Why didn't she knock and come in or slip the letter under my door and save on postage stamps? We'll never know, Fred and Marta."

"We won't, that's for sure," says Fred.

"Gee, it's been a long time we've been out here," Marta says.

The neighbor looks at his watch.

"Fred, Marta," he says, "look, it was my pleasure meeting you two and again, my condolences. I've got to get back to work. I'll excuse myself. I'm writing the story for publication."

"Good luck with it," Fred says. Together, he and Marta fumble with the lock to Margaret Markham's apartment, Number 23.

Once inside, the man next door realizes he has taken a chill. The hall was drafty, he thinks. He barely hears the Mardi Gras celebration now. Fred and

Marta next door are more noticeable. He hears a few thumps as though they're moving furniture. He hears them talking. Sitting down at the kitchen table, he looks out over the alley and begins to write in pencil on a legal sized pad:

I had egged her on by giving her the forecast she wanted. She'd made up her mind to hear it. I'd been thinking about her a few days and how I'd use her in a story of my own. Then I ended up using *her*! Calling her one night, I said, half in jest, "Yes, your story's over." She sighed and hung up. Now that hers is done, how shall I end my own story? Others she solicited are partly responsible for her fate, but I am mainly so....

He hears Fred and Marta raising their voices. Putting down the pencil, he reads what he has written, tears it up, throws it in the waste basket by his chair. With an empty glass to his ear, he proceeds to the wall. He can just make out Fred's yelling, but the words are indistinct. It's just Fred from Dallas, Texas, yelling.

I am waiting for a phone call from Margaret, he thinks. He checks to make sure the receiver is off the hook, even tries dialing himself. I am in a perfect hell of my own waiting for a telephone message from the sister and sister-in-law of the couple next door who are fighting in the kitchen near the gas stove. If I keep the phone tied up and off the hook, she won't get through to me. Not at first. Eventually she will, though, thinks the man next door. I'll let it ring a few dozen times, hoping it's a crank right up to the last. When the time comes it won't be. I'll pick up the receiver as I now do in practice and hear the patient voice, "Hello, I have a collect call from Miss or Mrs. Margaret Markham. Will you accept the charges?" I'll agree to pay for the call, but when the operator hangs up, I'll be left with nothing but the silence of years and miles, dead silences that finally decide to renew acquaintances.

GREAT SEA BATTLES

HE ASKED RAE-RITA TO RECONSIDER. He called her "honey-baby." When she said no he lowered his left foot over the side. The bow rested in mud and weeds, the aft-end in deeper water. The boat rocked slightly when he brought in his other foot. He had the outboard tilted up. "I hate the water," he said, crouching low on his way aft.

"Pull 'er up!" Rae-Rita said. Everything she said was an order. She couldn't ask in a nice voice, "Louis, could you please raise the sweet, faded flag of your surrender?" Or "Louis, could we go to the fish fry at the Holiday Inn on Friday, please?" No it was, "Pull 'er up! Pull up that durned flag and hurry, Louie!" or it was "We're going to the fish fry at the Holiday Inn Friday. So get ready for fish!"

Hands on her hips, she snapped her bubble gum.

"Ya, you go on," Ma added. "Give the flag a pull and show us how you've changed, Louie. Show us how you've reformed!"

He swore at them under his breath. Beside the motor, he'd propped up a willow branch. He hung a dingy pillowcase Ma'd given him to this willow branch. Dangling half in the water, it looked like the flag of a defeated man.

"Go on!" said Rae-Rita.

He grabbed the branch and raised up the flag. It ruffled slightly in the sweet, warm breeze, then kind of gave up and hung down.

I'd seen enough. Leaving them, I walked back through the railroad yard. Louie was shoving off with the paddle, and Ma and Rae-Rita crying and waving their hankies to him. It wasn't long before they got after me.

"Junior, why'nt you hitch up them trousers. All day long I get tired of seeing them dragging," Rae-Rita said between sobs. "I'm gonna miss your uncle"

"Junior, honey," Ma said, "see that you get your hair cut. And please don't come home tomorrow without it cut or I'll take the scissors out!"

"Yes, ma'am," I said.

We all took another look at Louie out on the bay. The water calm, his boat left a "v" in its wake.

When we got to the trailer court, I stayed outside to avoid Rae-Rita's orders. With Ma and Rae-Rita eating chocolates on the sofa, I was fairly safe. It was when they ran out or "The Edge of Night" ended that I had to watch for their orders. I brought out a kitchen chair and sat beneath the window in the little patch of yard that separated us from the neighbor's trailer. Through the kitchen window, which was propped partly open, I could hear them discussing uncle. We lived across from the court's laundry room. Listening to Ma, I could watch people coming and going and still be ready if she or Rae-Rita wanted me.

"All I can say is it's a good thing Louis never took to drinking," I heard Ma explaining, "not with his temperament. Rae-Rita honey, give me another of those creamy-filled candies, will you? I like the peanut-filled, too, don't you doubt that a minute, Rae-Rita! Which are *your* favorites by the way, Rae-honey? Le Bon-Bons, did you say?"

"Well, I like the cream-filled, too."

"Oh, my mistake," Ma said. "Then you take this one."

"No, you."

"But, honey, I have to watch my schoolgirl figure," Ma said and laughed. "Both of us gals do. But you not as much. Of course, you're younger. That's an advantage. And you've got to keep yourself up for when Louie returns from that — what did he call it?"

"Voyage of Penance," I yelled.

"Voyage of Penance … yes, you've got to look good and keep up that figure, Rae."

"You know, Louie's the kind of temperament," Rita-Rae said, "that can't get control of himself. If he likes something, there's no stopping him, but he's got to have it. He was that way with me. I guess that's his 'lack of self-control.' Hand me another of the Fanny Farmer's. I'll try a peanut-filled this time. No, give me a 'caramel cluster.' Then let's us open the Brach's box to see what that candy company offers two lonely ladies."

"Here you are, honey," Ma said. "I got a catalogue from the new store that opened over at the mall. It's for big and tall gals … store called 'The Ample Lady.' You know it's over next to Carma Lou's 'House of Magic.'"

"Across from the candy shop?" Rae-Rita asked.

"How'd ya know?" I asked.

"About Louie's lack of self-control," Rae-Rita went on as if not to hear, "this is the best way to break him of his habits. Get him out on the bay away from the occasion of sin a trailer court provides. Get him out and keep him there. We cain't afford any fancy 'rest cures' like them movie stars or what not. As long as he's willing, this ain't going to cost us and might-could cure him. What were you saying about 'Ample Ladies' by the way?" she asked. "You calling me ample?"

"No, no, Rae-Rita … Boy!" Ma yelled.

"Right here, Ma and Rae-Rita."

"Junior, seeing you're now the man around here," she said, "You get your Mama and me some ginger snaps!"

"And, honey," said Ma, "bring us the soda crackers and each a bottle of Nehi grape."

Once they'd give me an order to fill, they'd kind of forget me for awhile.

"I was saying it's lack of self-control causes him — causes *us*! — such trouble with Louis."

"But you know, Rae-Rita, honey, if it's anyone could straighten him out, it's

34

you. Who else do you think he's setting out there for? Here's a man who sets in a motorboat for as long as it takes to break himself of bad habits. 'Get thee behind me, Satan! Take your temptation away!' Now I'd say that's a compliment to you, honey."

Strips of cellophane tape kept Rae-Rita's forehead curls in place. She'd smeared her mouth with pink lipstick. Embarrassed by Ma's saying it, she blushed and dabbed her face with a powder puff.

I brought in their order from the kitchen. "Your Nehis and ginger snaps, ladies," I said. But Ma complained. "You know I like the 'Lo-Cal' grape, son."

As the day wore on, I figured Louie'd return later. He'd approach Ma, me, and Rae-Rita through the mist, his 4-horse Johnson-Mertz a low purr against the croaking frogs. "I'm here to win," he'd announce to us, and I'd be happy he was back. "I've got a system of how to put the Lord to work dealing cards for me," he'd say. I dreamt Louie'd change clothes real fast, wave good-bye and be out the door to some card game in the court.

"He has a gambling man's misery," Rae-Rita would say and shake her head sadly.

"What he makes at work he loses," Ma'd cry.

So maybe it *was* good he was out there. I thought maybe that's where he belonged. I grew to like the idea of his chasing out demons. The bay was the best place to wrestle with Satan, to wring your hands and weep for Jesus' sake.

"Louie has to lose himself to find himself," Ma'd say. "When there's no shameful, sinful card-play around, salvation has a chance."

Through my window at night, I'd hear moaning, hollering and crying, such noises coming up from the bay as you've never heard. There was the gnashing of teeth and wailing of a man going through hell.

My uncle had a tent aboard. He'd put it up at night or if it rained. For a month and a half, he stayed out rocking on the waters, and I thought it was all for Rae-Rita, the former Douglas County Honey Bee Queen. Then one morning when he edged up to a stump and propped his paddle in the mud I began to suspect him.

"Did you sleep last night? You look grand for a sinner," I said.

"I slept some, I guess."

"You'll be coming in soon, please won't you, uncle?"

"Well, there are things to figure out first, son. If you need me, I'm always close in here around the swamp or bay with my lines strung watching the stars." He tossed me the fish he'd caught. "Can you keep a secret?"

"I sure can."

He hadn't shaved yet. He rubbed his jaw and began laughing.

"Journey of penance, hey? ... Whew, I'm dry." He reached for a bottle of brown water.

"I can get you some fresh."

"This water came out of the swamp. Some of the trailer court boys been visitin' me."

He took a sip, closed it. Then he got real pale — maybe from the boat, the heat of the day, or the contaminated water. He lost the look of the "anointed," the look of Grace Abounding Ma says you get when you're holy. Pulling out the paddle, he pushed his boat out and headed for deeper water. He has reasons for sailing early, I figured. Later I'd bring him supplies.

I saw him off and went home sad and confused about his behavior, so that it was going on two months, and Rae-Rita kept saying between snapping her gum, "He'll really cure himself. I bet he never touches another playing card. Not him. He ain't but doin' it for me. I'm so happy I might run for Miss Honey Bee again." And Ma would say, "Now Remember, Rae-Rita, he's still a sick man out there."

"You ain't kidding, Bess. Sixty days, by gosh. He sure must love me after all."

Then, because I was their servant, they'd start in. "Junior, please get the Wasa bread for your Ma so she can have her lunch and watch her shows. She's had such a terrible morning. And I got a laundry load in over across the street. Can you possibly see about it if you've got free time, honey boy?"

But then one day, the sixty-first of Uncle Louie's great sea battles, Ma got this brainstorm. Possibly it came after I told her how good, happy, and healthy he looked when I saw him. Possibly it was the way the sun slanted off the porch roof. Who knows? Maybe it gave her heatstroke and changed her way of thinking. But she got the idea that maybe, just maybe, Uncle Louie *wanted* to be out there, that no matter what we did he wouldn't come out of the water. Pulling off her glasses, she said, "Rae-Rita, sixty-one odd days is enough for anyone to find his peace, don't you agree?"

In a minute, we were out the door, down the path, and across the tracks. We didn't see him out there. Ma pointed her fists and screwed up her face trying to figure out where he could be. Then, after a long wait, I saw him come from the swamp over a ways from where we were. He didn't appear to notice us, and Ma and Rae-Rita commenced hollering and threatening. It was getting toward evening. We built a fire with driftwood. Then the mosquitoes forced our retreat uphill to the court. Ma and Rae-Rita coaxed themselves home to a box of Fanny Farmers, which made it easier to stay in for the night.

It went on like that, Uncle Louie out there oblivious to our efforts, until the end of the week. Ma and Rae-Rita were just fuming. Word had got around the trailer court that Louie refused to come in off the bay. The other trailer court gals came over to Ma, mine, and Rae-Rita's place for coffee and doughnuts.

"My own husband's been acting strange, too, Bess and Rae," said Mrs. Bates. She lived in an end trailer.

"And mine!" said another lady.

"You know how they all think of Louie, Bess," said Mrs. Jenkins, "how they always follow him around, how the fellows can't ever seem to do without him."

(I heard the gals agreeing from where I sat outside in the yard.)

"I'll be darned," said Ma.

Then Mrs. Purcell piped in: "You give 'em booze and the bunch of fools will desert any woman!"

"Booze?" Ma asked.

By then I could tell she and Rae-Rita were really steamed. Ma called Aunt Birdie on the phone. I could hear her shouting, "He's traded one sin in for another, Bird, and now I don't believe he's ever planning to come in off that boat ... call Hattie," Ma said.

Birdie called Hattie, her sister, who lives in the next trailer court over; and Hattie called Mrs. Wayne Wright; and Wayne Wright, Isabelle Hill; and Isabelle Hill, Mrs. Thomas — until all the girls and relations knew about it that Louie wasn't coming back any time soon.

The first thing next morning when it got light, we were down there —Rae-Rita, me, Ma, Hattie, Birdie, Sally Jenkins — all of them. We were there confronting Uncle Louie. When he saw us, he was cruising downshore past the swamp by an old willow which'd washed up into the bay last spring.

He angled to us on the shore, all along, sneaky-like, eyeing us up, for when Rae-Rita, Ma, and them trailer court gals started in hollering to high heavens, just as slow as you please he made that wide arcing circle I'd seen him practicing out there all week, and grinning, shook his hat and headed out for deeper water. Hooting and cussing, turning the boat for all she was worth, he appeared like a giant in the pocket telescope I brought along. He put his hands to his nose and, wiggling his fingers, made a funny gesture at Rae-Rita and Ma, so that Ma yelled, "You're a spiteful creature, Louie, but don't for a moment think the Lord above is not watching! You won't go boating on the Lake of Fire, Louie! There ain't no U-turns on the Road to Hell!" She rolled up her pantlegs in her frenzy and began wading out right through the mud and sticks and weeds.

Still he went round and round, veering in at us, scaring the be-Jesus out of Ma as he did, then shooting out farther than before, all the while tilting some contaminated drinking water to his mouth, and smiling and waving the crazy white flag in defiance. It was the same white flag as before only prouder now in his strong sailor's hands. Then I myself began contemplating a career at sea. In front of everybody, in front of all the trailer court gals, I took a fit of laughter when I imagined myself in a sailor's suit with my hat tipped forward. It was the white flag and the boat I liked so much. In the telescope, I could see them ever so plainly until Rae-Rita took away the spyscope and folded it up.

"You've got no business being with respectable ladies," she said. She pulled me over away from the others. "You're with us or against us now, for we're all of us here respectable. Choose sides fast, Junior ... Your Ma and me, or that" — She pointed out to where Louie was rocking the boat — "that drunken sailor!"

"Hey, Junior," he yelled and held up the bottle. "Anchors Aweigh!" His voice travelled clearly over the water. When Rae-Rita made a grab for me, I broke loose of her. Kicking off my shirt and tennis shoes, I made it through the pack of them and into the water. I passed Ma going out. Her clothes soaked, water dripping from her hair, she was wading in. Some weeds hung off her one ear, the starboard ear. As I glided past, knifing through the water, she glared at me and tried to say something, but only murky water came out of her mouth now. She sputtered and gave up, unaccustomed to the ways of the sea, I guess.

Then it was just me — an able-bodied seaman — still laughing, heading out toward the cool depths and safety of Uncle Louie's boat. Half-way out, I could already hear him piping me aboard.

HARRY AND THE DANCER

FOR THE MONEY, THE HOTEL is agreeable enough, especially with the bridge lights scanning its wooden front. At such times you can see how it means good harbor to a traveller, someone coming to town late at night in the fog. There are many who have come here that way.

But the manager of a dancing troupe does not think of such things. He will not notice the bridge lights shading the sides of the building blue, nor care about the spacious lobby or array of potted plants in silver vases. It is his job to cut costs where he may. That is why the manager of the dancing troupe chose the Armitage.

Harry, the keeper of the hotel, had planned for this. In spring he sent a letter offering services at a moderate price. By the first day of summer, he was well under way fixing up the Armitage and its appointments. After apologizing to the consumptives on the upper floors for disturbing them, he set about retiling the foundations of their bidets, telling his boarders not to wash their feet in them once the dancers came.

In addition, he hung rose lampshades in the hallways and festooned each door with garlands of ivy.

Along the balustrade over the lobby, he wound bright crepe. And to make the furniture inviting, he stuffed the springs back in the chairs and swept the satin arms with a whisk broom.

Finally, and though it was a breach of trust, he rid himself of the ladies who slipped in after midnight.

Yet a person lodging in a quality hotel might expect such preparation. What Harry sought for the Armitage was the individual touch, something of which the Quincy and the Blue Rondo couldn't boast. He sought one of those extras that could make a place distinctive and elegant.

When he hit upon it, he knew he had something unique. With an entire dancing show camped on his upper floors and leg-weary from conditioning drills, his new invention would come in handy every day. What he proposed was the result of a philosophy he had developed while staying in waterfront hotels. He knew the disadvantages of such places: tenuous walls that allowed for all manner of noises; night deskmen who would refuse you a clock. Those places, they were not clean. The owners did very little to please. But the Armitage Arms would be different.

Half-way up from the lobby, Harry began his invention. Where the bannister and stairs met to form a right angle, he secured a pulley from the ceiling. Through this pulley he strung twine, guiding it over the potted plants and the shredded leather couch directly to the desk, at which end rested an empty wicker fruit basket, the ascent of this basket governed by a curious metal crank of Harry's own making. For the convenience of his customers, he could, with such a system, sweep parcels half-way to the second floor. An ingenious method. A parcel post, he thought.

Even more important was what so many places forgot: the lodger's right to privacy. Upon this Harry insisted, so often in the years when he was homeless had his own privacy been interrupted. Not enough personal privacy existed in the world as it was. Nor did these invasions of privacy always occur in the hotel rooms he took. In city parks as he wandered alone, out of the fog would come strangers. From public buildings, subways, alleys, doorfronts, they strolled toward him. "Dark night, eh?" they'd whisper. Anything to start a conversation. By the ship canal, lonely intruders tried to see him in their matchglow. They tried shedding light on him, on who he was. He wasn't, thank God, one of the lonely. This was when he was young and could only dream of managing a hotel. He went to the park, the canal, even the movie house during matinees to be alone with his hotel thoughts. He wished to sit untroubled and anonymous in back rows of downtown movie houses. Preparing for the dancers, Harry kept this in mind: how in parks, movie houses and hotel rooms, his privacy had been invaded — a tapping, a faint rustling of keys, the pinched face of the desk clerk realizing his mistake. At Harry's, however, a guest room was to be sacred, inviolate above all else.

To insure the dancing troupe's privacy, Harry warned his permanent residents how to act. Most of them were too sick to care. It was a tubercular ward on the third floor of Harry's. All one could hear was the constant shuffling of slippers and an occasional rasp of air. In addition, Harry changed all the locks on the second floor rooms where the dancers would be staying. He made sure the doors were sturdy and the bolts easily fastened. He held the only keys to the rooms and at night he locked them in his cupboard. Then one day a properties van and bus stood in the fog before the Armitage. Bold letters on the side of the bus announced: ZGODA TROUPE, EASTERN EUROPEAN DANCE. Through the upstairs window, Harry spied a young man hunched over the steering wheel of the van, the door flung wide. "They're here!" Harry called, then realized he was speaking to himself.

He raced downstairs, dressed in a black suit and red tie, which he'd recently gotten back from the cleaners. This was Harry's chance. To him it was not simply a busload of entertainers, but an *opportunity*. To succeed here would say countless things about him and the Armitage Arms Hotel. It would be the first great triumph of his life. Up to now he hadn't done well in life. But then, he thought, he'd never managed such a fine hotel as this.

The bus doors slammed open. Among a group of young dancers, Harry spotted the manager, a man with a gray moustache and an attache case in his hands. Together Harry and his guest strolled in, talking of the weather before taking care of the dancers' accomodations. Harry fidgeted behind the reservation desk, hoping the man would question the wicker fruit basket's uses.

Within an hour, Harry had the dancing troupe's members assigned to rooms. The manager thanked him. It was good, thought Harry, that he'd seen to things in advance of their arrival. His self-doubts began to vanish. By supper hour, he was pleased with his day. He allowed himself a small glass of wine, some cheese, some crackers, then tea. As the water for his tea bubbled and he dreamed happily of how he'd been taking hotel rooms near the waterfront for thirty years, he heard something at the desk. For a second he wondered if he should shut off the stove. Shaking the crumbs from his shirt, he held aside the curtain and entered the lobby.

"I missed the others in Perdido," she said. "I looked away and the bus was gone. It's that driver."

She was uncertain of herself, Harry saw; her eyes on the floor averted his. In spite of this, he thought she was attractive in an awkward way, the type of woman he would expect to be included in an Eastern European dance troupe. To come with the bags she had, she must be strong, thought Harry. He checked the register.

"Here is a single room," he said. He would lodge her on the third floor. He was around the desk in an instant, her bags heavier than he'd expected.

Approaching the second floor, holding tight to the bannister, she broke her silence and inquired about the twine and the pulley below her and where they went. He wouldn't have expected it. "What a good idea," she said. He gave her the room he once slept in, a dingy room which looked out on the wharf. Before the room's one, dusty window squatted a radiator, its paint flaking in spots. He set her bags next to it. A dresser and nightstand stood on one side of the room, above the dresser a mirror whose glass was streaked and yellow. A coverlet atop the narrow bed in the room's center bore spots where an unsteady pensioner had dropped his cough medicine. The bed took up most of the room whose other appointments consisted of a framed painting of a winter scene on the wall and a faded divan, a kind of loveseat, which to anyone but Harry would appear incongruous in such a setting.

"I hope you enjoy yourself," he said and bowed his way out.

Later, he could not help checking for her name. He shuffled through the guest register, remembered how she'd stood just opposite him and how he'd looked at her when her head was bowed. He'd looked and looked for the longest time. He found in the register that her name was Hedwig.

In bed he thought of her, too. That afternoon, she had seemed to sense how it was with him. He had the unsettling feeling that she knew just what he'd been doing with his life; what he was all about, for instance, here in a hotel by the water. Never had he known anyone like this. Never had he been so shaken meeting anyone.

He was better in the morning. He had slept soundly. He had his coffee, and there was the business of the hotel to see about. The dancers were out. They had arranged to take their breakfasts down the street, then go directly to practice, remaining until late afternoon, so the place was clear and it stayed that way while he got his work done.

Then for two or three weeks, he failed to see her, and though he'd not forgotten her, he managed to regain his composure. Funny how it had happened in the first place, he thought, how she had upset him like that. It was the way she looked.

Because she never received any parcels from home like the others, he had even stopped going through the mail when it arrived, although the other dancers regularly came to the second floor for mail after practice.

It was mere coincidence, just in the nature of things that his comings and goings did not coincide with hers, he thought. Yet he was watching for her lately and wondering how it was he hadn't seen her. It was foolish of him, he supposed. What was she, after all, but a dancer with whom he exchanged a few words on the way upstairs to her room. How he would have loved sending her mail by the pulley.

When he did see her again, she stopped one afternoon and waved to him, but he, unable to move, stood there beside the desk, yelling something to her about the rainy, foggy weather and how she did not have to fear for her privacy at the Armitage.

All this time, in spite of how he brooded, he kept along with his work, so that the place seemed tidier than ever. He shuddered seeing the evenings pass and found himself polishing the brass fixtures on the third floor later each day. After this second time, he did not see her, and he grew more anxious. They have no rules against such things, so she has probably taken a lover, he thought. It drove him wild wondering. For a moment, he even hated living in hotels. Sometimes they offered too much privacy. They isolated people. Who but an isolated person would lodge in a waterfront hotel in the first place? Hedwig had other dancers to look after her; she had the troupe for support, he thought. But whom did he have but a hotel full of pensioners with failing lungs?

Later and later he stayed up, peering around corners, uncertain that she wasn't already in her room. He even took to sliding sheets of paper under her door. In the mornings he would check to see if they had been moved. They were always there. No change had occurred through the night.

Wrapped in a soiled woolen blanket which he took from the cot behind the front desk, he began to spend an occasional night on three stairs next to her room, stairs leading to a supply closet where he kept mops and disinfectants of various types. By sitting here, he could not miss her return. Throwing the blanket around himself, he arrived at his post well after midnight. On the tiled steps, he would lean against the wall and doze until some old pensioner stumbled his way to the bathroom, more dead than alive. At such times, the hacking and coughing quieted. Among the old, someone afoot at that hour was cause for alarm. In rooms up and down the hall of the hotel, old, sick men clutched wallets and coin purses and suppressed their own dry coughs.

Harry had no cough. He took care of himself. Hearing the Armitage creak in the wind or hearing a taxi screech outside as it hurried away from the neighborhood, he'd look up, wishing for Hedwig's return. He brought another blanket and a pillow one night. No one cared what Harry did on the third floor. They'd given up hope. They simply wanted to stay put out of the fog.

Harry stared at the door — his and Hedwig's, he liked to think. In all the world, he'd seen no such door. Both it and its frame were painted deep brown to match the faded beige of the walls. Furthermore, the door was scarred. Toward the bottom, heel marks, perhaps Harry's own, discolored the deep brown paint. Some consumptive, it appeared, had etched his mark in the door before dying, or perhaps it was Harry: parallel lines carved in the wood. Once painted over, their trails were still noticeable. They ran five inches straight up the door to the brass number — three numbers — each held by a screw near its center.

The door separated him, kept him out of his room. From his *chaise* on the supply closet stairs, he saw only part of the door. To get the full view, he needed to stand directly before it as he did each night now, the blanket wound around his shoulders. Those who rose for the bathroom exchanged no pleasantries with Harry.

The door consisted of two rectangular panels set in from the rest. They stood above and below a kind of centerboard, which protruded perhaps a half-inch. From the right of the centerboard and halfway down from the top a tarnished brass doorknob stuck out.

Harry found himself very late one night peering through the keyhole below the doorknob, but finding nothing. He should have remembered, he thought to himself, how he'd plugged it on the other side when he'd occupied the room himself. Seeking privacy, he'd placed a one-half inch square of black tape over the inside keyhole. As far as he could see into the hole, there was nothing but dust — that and the kind of darkness he truly feared. A blackness worse than the huge, old movie house's blackness was concentrated there in the keyhole of Hedwig's room. He would bet that on the other side of the door, on the other side of that vast darkness in the keyhole, was a room transformed, a beautiful, sunlit place. No doubt, thought Harry, she has stuffed the coverlet beneath the bed and replaced it with a counterpane from home. No doubt she has brought curtains scented with lavender and, from the florist, a bouquet for the nightstand.

Just after 4 a.m., he returned to the lobby. But that night he came back up. Placing his pillow on the supply closet's steps and with the old, soiled blanket around him, he pretended to polish the brass fixtures on the third floor. He worked ten minutes on the fire extinguisher, then, returning it to its glass and metal case, he turned to the doorknobs and room numbers. He kept particular watch over the door which stood in the middle of the hallway near the supply closet: a door eight feet by three in length and width and one- and one-half inches thick, Hedwig's. He ran his hands over it. He felt the doorknob and peered into the keyhole — dust and darkness. On his knees, he lowered his head to peek at the paper strips he'd been leaving under the door. He recalled once long ago how the door had locked by itself. The locksmith later said it wasn't the lock, strangely, but the mechanism inside the lock's housing causing the problem. Part of it had fallen in such a way as to jam the lock. It wasn't the lock, but the mechanism. With his polishing cloth and a can of Brasso, Harry rubbed the plate beneath the doorknob where lay the mechanism which once caused the problem. He returned to the lobby much later that night and fell asleep on his cot.

He polished the brass of the three-story hotel each night for several weeks, and each time he came upstairs, he thought of the mechanism which was buried in the lock's housing, waiting perhaps to trip again. The cold, metal secrets of such mechanisms amazed him. He could not get them out of his head. Wherever he looked, he imagined them working in perfect mechanical precision. He thought: each turn of a doorknob will move the mechanism inside, however slightly. He lived in a world of catches and cylinders now and the keys which locked or released them. Sometimes, their cold angularity favored him; square and circle granted his wishes. He'd dream of doors swinging open. He'd see all such secret mechanisms in working order. But other times bolts sprang shut, allowing no hope. It was a world of steel mysteries where Harry was not entirely comfortable. Still, he returned to gaze into the keyhole or speculate on the secrets of the mechanism in the door lock, the mechanism of darkness and exclusion. It was as if this door alone had come to symbolize the times he'd been separated from others, or defeated.

Harry recalled as a child his stepmother's door being closed to him briefly on Saturdays, or a church door once being shut against him. He saw the choir loft lit up and heard them practicing, but the mechanism in the door had apparently slipped shut on him when he had every right to be inside where his stepmother sent him. The best he could do that time was hum along outside. He began to sing as it got colder, until finally he was actually hollering against the night and their singing. He'd been shut out again more recently, this time from a downtown movie house where he'd gone, as he so often did, to dream away an afternoon. Pulling on the door, he'd found it shut fast. Then he looked up. FOR SALE, said the marquee. The place was closed forever; and just beyond reach that incredible, deep privacy waiting for him.

Doors meant privacy, that's all. They put an end to something, to openness and companionship, he thought. You couldn't just walk in when a door was shut to you. Always something had to end during such exchanges, someone had to lose and most often it had been he, Harry. He imagined all of the Armitage's doors thrown wide so that he could choose where to go. What were the keyholes that they should keep him so lonely? What was this darkness?

On the afternoon of what was to be Hedwig's last day at the Armitage, however, Harry's true perspective returned, and it was painful to him: he was alone in the Armitage Arms Hotel with the springs and bolts of its doors. His whole hotel had for too long been a private pleasure to him. He'd gone for the wicker basket and come back with bread and wine. He brought four or five bouquets of plastic flowers from the lobby as well. He could not help himself then and, before he knew it, he was past the threshold, stealing into the third floor room. How different it might have been if she, Hedwig, had opened it and said, "Please come in, Harold." But she hadn't. As far as he could determine, she hadn't been here in a month.

If it was bright though shabby in the hallway, the place lit by several naked lightbulbs hanging down from the ceiling, inside her room it was dark, the shade drawn. On the dresser lay a hair brush, a bottle of shampoo, a face towel, and a lace-trimmed undergarment; tucked into a corner of the mirror, a glossy photo of some matinee idol or other Harry vaguely recalled seeing at the Bel-Rio. There was the loveseat, too, What surprised him most was that the bed in the room had not been made. The old coverlet was thrown back, the sheets mussed. He'd always wanted to go back to a simpler time, a time without doors like that on Hedwig's room, where he could rest outside in a bed of flowers, drink his wine, eat the bread, and call to the pretty maidens dancing in the forest night, but this was not at all as he expected. The room was bleak and dingy. In the past month or so, dust had accumulated on windowsill and radiator — blown in from the harbor coal docks — and the paint on the radiator flaked in large pieces, some of which had fallen to the floor.

He tucked in the white sheet. With his hands, he smoothed the coverlet, then straightened items on the dresser. With his pocket comb, he pulled hair from her brush. He threw the hair into the wastebasket. On the dresser, he replaced the brush, bristles up. The face towel he folded carefully, too, and placed beside it. He also straightened the photo in the mirror. Then he placed the flowers around. One other obligation remained to be performed. He turned to the door which did not fit quite perfectly in its frame. At the top it slanted downward perhaps a quarter-inch. This did not concern Harry, as much as the door's hinge pins did. Holding the edge of the waste basket to the knob of the uppermost pin, he forced the pin up and out. The other upper hinge pin he pulled out as well. With the lower two he did the same, then lifted the door — number 309 — off its hinges and propped it in the hallway. This done, he sat on the bed, legs over the side. Then he tried the loveseat. He opened his wine, cut off a piece of bread and cheese. Eating and drinking, he must have stayed in the loveseat an hour or so, for when he rose slowly to welcome evening and release more doors from hinge and frame, the first dancers were returning from their performance.

"Where's the wicker basket?" they were calling from the second floor. "Harry, where are you and your wicker basket?"

But Harry was no longer quick to oblige them.

He heard their voices on the landing now, heard them over the coughing of the tenants. The dancers were coming near until finally they stood just outside looking at the door he'd removed to allow free passage to Hedwig's room.

"Come in," he called from the loveseat. They were standing there pointing at him and giggling. Disgusted, some of them turned and left.

"Don't go so soon. Help me finish the wine at least. Then we'll open all the rooms like this one and have a dance-party."

They weren't staying around long, however. They'd take a look and leave. Harry heard someone saying that he'd better notify the manager of the dancing troupe, then Hedwig, whose room it was, then perhaps even the police. But through it all, through all the insults and giggling, Harry of the Armitage sat very privately with wine and bread in the meadow of plastic flowers.

ROUTE OF THE ZEPHYRS

IT'S DIRTY IN THE MILLWORKS. I like to hear things around me going full-force — the motors and presses ... the way they bang. I don't wear earplugs, not me, thanks. No earplugs for me. The noise and dirty air make me feel A-OK.

"How's the wife?" Gordy yells in the boiler room. He's got cotton in his ears.

"They're cutting her hours down at the cafe," I holler.

"Wha—?""

"Her hours, they're cutting her hours!"

"Ha, you oughta hear what they did to mine ... laid her off, told her g'night. Now she's got no benefits. Four months and they lay her off. How do you figure it?

I take the cotton out of Gordy's left ear and cup my hand to it.

"Well, what about mine?" I ask. "Ain't that something, how they cut her hours? What we got to live on besides my pay?"

"It sure is," he says, nodding. "She's some tomato, your wife," he yells and stokes the boiler with coal. I think of her and my head starts to spin. The engine room's dirty air makes me sneeze and the noise (clanging, oh, screeching) puts me in a happy mood.

Hopping the man-lift, I ride up to second floor where Augie, the boss, is checking the conveyor belt. It's so loud I have to yell over the dirty, crazy air up there.

Hey, they took Gordy up to the hospital."

"What 't hell now?"

"Gettin' a drink of water."

"Yeah?"

"Toilet seat fell on his head! Ha!"

"It ain't quittin' time yet, Beany, and you ain't funny," he says.

Walt Tessler's up here, too. He's gripping a timber beam like he'd pull the whole damn place down if he could. He just stands there squeezing the beam, gritting his teeth: his wife went nuts on him and left with a truck driver, his wife he loves. "She ran up long distance phone bills on me, too," he says. Now all he does is squeeze this beam for eight hours like he'd pull the mill apart. He squeezes so hard his face and hands grow white.

See ya later, Walter," I say. "Don't let it get to ya."

I walk away so he can't see me. Sneaking back, I tap his right shoulder, then duck to the left. When he turns, he don't see nobody. His pain-grin gets worse.

Over in East-wing, Emil Sandvick's having trouble with his teen-agers.

"Hey, Emiliano," I say.

"Hey, Beany," he says. "What'd I hear about your old lady hitting you with a bowling ball after league play Tuesday night?"

"S'true," I say. "Smashed my fingers good for me when she got home." (The nails are coming off my fingers.)

"Hey," Emil asks, "why don't you ever wear a mask or earplugs?"

"I like the dirty air and noise, especially the noise," I say. "Hear about Gordy downstairs by the way? He was getting a drink of water...."

After work, I stop at the Tappa-Keg tavern and stand around awhile.

"Hey, Beany," the guys call.

"Hey, you guys," I say.

There's that drunk teacher was in here the other night. He sees me, calls me "Weenie."

"It's not Weenie," I say.

Later on, half past nine o'clock, I roll in to the parking lot of the apartment house. You'd think she'd have something ready for my supper, but I have to fix my own while my wife sits there smoking a Lucky and looking through a magazine. Some ashes land on her. When I come in, she don't look up.

"Where'd you go today?" I ask her. "How come you're home so early?"

"—got a ride."

"With who?"

"Someone is all," she says.

I've got something behind the couch which I pull out to look at after work. I cradle it in my arms, then slide it back in. She don't pay attention to me.

Electric trains are a hobby, too, "Route of the Zephyrs" being my favorite. I keep O-gauge track around the apartment — fifteen feet of track in the front room, more in the hallway and bedroom.

"My railroad watch, where is it?" I ask. I go back in the bedroom. "How do you expect me to operate without a railroad watch?"

"No! You gonna play with them damn trains tonight? Why don't you just clean the bazooka for a change?"

"Never mind. Watch your p's and q's," I tell her. Hey, I hear ticking sounds from her underwear on the bed — my watch, she's hidden it there. I look over and see the pink pillow with heart stitched on it! TRUE LOVE, BEANY & HANNA.

In the living room again, I move the transformer. I hear electricity, smell the dirty air. The electric train starts slow from where I left it last night. It gets itself going when I move the transformer to Fast. My R.R. watch reads 10:03 p.m. I can sit and watch the train. She's almost gone round the living room once already. I don't sleep for thinking of him upstairs and the dirty air at work. The man upstairs is noisy. He does my wife Hanna in the daytime. I know it, and I hate the air because of him. That's why I go around without a mask and earplugs. I like to breathe the hot, close, dirty air. My trains give me rest. They're my hobby. I get two working together. I miss the noise of men with a mission.

Why do I hear things in my head? I turn off the trains. Upstairs, I hear him walking, pacing. I hear him cough and sputter, hear his coffee pot going, hear him wiggle the handle of the toilet to keep it from running. I know one or two squeaks on the bedroom ceiling mean something in my wife's and his code language. I think they mean something like: "Let's have another good time when ol' Weiner-Beaner goes to work tomorrow."

"Hanna, get me that pink satin pillow!" I yell to the bedroom where she's fixing for sleep.

I pull my recorded train sounds out of the record cabinet. I turn the hi-fi up loud. You have to watch out or the Route will fly off the tracks. The record's scratchy. Fuzz on the needle makes me irritable. All of a sudden, I'm in an ugly way. Dirty air and pistons pulling, I need to hear the steel metal screech. I have smoke pellets, so oh, my trains look good and fine. You should hear the hi-fi and see it shaking it's on so loud and then the part with the whistle.

She brings the pillow. I see the heart and rip it open before her eyes.

"Stop that!" she yells.

I throw the torn heart away.

She's got some antique eyeglasses her Gramma wore. Round, pinched, small specs like you've never seen, they've got dark brown frames. I wear them for the dizziness they bring on. When she's gone back in the bedroom, I put them on and get mad. I can't see right with them; everything's a blur.

"No, that's a 'hair-loom,' " she says when she returns from sending some code language upstairs.

I put them on again to show her. Sick and dizzy, I pick up the blurred stuffing from my torn heart. I look crazy with these small, round glasses on.

"Come on here," I say. "You've got something, a spot or something on your blouse there."

I put my fingers to it. Tricked, she looks down. My fingers flicking up to her lips and nose.

"Real funny, Beany," she says, her face a blur.

"I got no heart for you, Hanna. The way you've been doing me with the guy upstairs, I've got nothing but a torn-heart."

"I got nothing for you either, Bean-Brain Beany! And never did!"

She goes back to the bedroom while I reach for a sharp pencil off the table, prop it point up between the two couch cushions, and yell for her "to come on back here."

"Now here, sit down and let's talk," I tell her, guiding her to the couch. She sees it.

"You fool," she says. "You stubborn, old fool."

Upstairs, I hear him pace back and forth. With my telescope, I will shoot down the stars through the ceiling, see the moon through my bazooka.

"What're you doing?" she asks.

WHACK! my hand tells her.

I'm hell on the transformer, a telescope between my legs. Connected, that's me.

"WHO-e-e-e-e-O-O-O!" the train yells as it comes round the bend by the recliner-rocker.

She's holding her hand to where I smacked her. "Get out of here and take your ragged heart with you!" she yells.

Bazooka, my love, you're a lightweight, hollow tube. Effective range for aimed fire: 800 to 2,000 yards and capable of blowing 4-inch holes in armor plate.

Bazooka, my love, I pull you out from behind the couch. Holding you in my arms, I swing you carelessly this way and that. Down on one knee I aim my dirty noise up at the ceiling. I have my shells in the closet and my dirty air.

Bazooka, my love, I bang you accidentally on the walls in the hallway. I am near tears to feel the back-blast of your hollow tube.

"You come out, neighbor!" I yell when I get upstairs.

Down the hall Mrs. Kominski, the landlady, sticks her beak out. I scare her. "Oh, my God, he's got a bazooka!" she shrieks and ducks back in. His telephone is ringing, the man upstairs. Is Hanna, my wife with the recently slapped face, calling to warn her lover-boy? Is she downstairs ringing him up? What is their code language? Have I finally caught the two at their own game? (Oh, Hanna, you worked at a cafe with three names where the truck drivers came, but you favored me!) Over the phone is she pleading with him, "Quick, rinse off the cologne I gave you before he smells it!" What in hell kind of first name is Murray anyway?

His door's shut. Murray in the apartment directly above me, I have scared you half out of your wits. Murray, I am outside your door now. Murray, I'm getting closer. "Go watch test patterns!" I holler.

Bazooka, down with you I go, carrying your love, banging you along the way. Mrs. Kominski is hollering above me: "He's got a bazooka, for Christ sakes! Did you see it?"

In the laundry room, I load you up and fall on my knees to witness your armor-piercing strength. With a terrible roar, you show your anger and tear through a Maytag, a Sears Kenmore and three helpless dryers. You shred their armor, leave them wounded and dripping suds.

I have Gramma's glasses on. I hop in the car. I head for the shops on the north side of town. Somebody on a bike ahead. I swerve, hit the horn, roll down the window and shout.

Slowing for the light: green and red and yellow, green and red. I hate signals. I hate the code language I don't know. She's a waitress over on 3rd. I breathe the dirty air. Through my glasses I breathe it and get good and dizzy. That noise of your back-blast is all right with me. How do I look with my glasses on? Have they discovered the Maytag in the laundry room? Are the suds building? Four shells left. "Toilet seat fell on his head!" That's a good one.

I scrape the curb. I run over a beer bottle, hear it crunching. I open the door, climb out, shoulder a bazooka whose tube is five feet long, green inside and out. It's going to sound like war. I slam the winged shell in. Salvation. Nummi Jewelers. Outreach Mission and Assembly Hall. Berger Hardware. Bridgeman's Ice Cream Store. Salvation. Marcus Sporting Goods. Anchor Bar. Tip-Top Tavern. 5th St. Hotel. Berger Hardware. Salvation Army. Cedar Lounge. Salvation.

"Stop!" I yell, feeling her kick, the winged messenger rushing forth, the flash and walls exploding.

I quick pack the bazooka in the trunk again. Bricks falling, a fire starts. With the old gramma's specs everything's blurred. I hear the screaming that can't be too serious or it would stop. I gave a shell to the ribs of the building. Beany says, "Bazooka Hello!" He's on his way. The smell of the assault in his nose.

The dirty air heads up 5th where the laughing sirens call. No one's seen me. Back there doesn't know what hit. But the noise and the crazy, dirty air of work stay.

At the Q.T., I say to the bartender, "Hey!"

"Hey."

I drink a beer. "Want one?"

"No."

"Gimme a six-pack to go."

"Sure, Beany. Nice glasses."

I like it fine, that cannon in the trunk.

"Look at my heart. Does it look O.K. to you?" I ask him.

News is on the radio. Hey, how are the trains back home running and the "Route" especially? Hey, how is my torn pillow-heart? I think it is on the mend. I'll pay for the Maytag's armor. I won't mind. (Hanna, I think I'm mending.)

I drink the beer in the car, all six of them. Mrs. Kominski and the loverboy got a good scare. Ha, Murray, see if you come fooling around with Hanna now that I've got my bazooka out.

I drive to the west side. Come back, driving slow, enjoying a beer. Sit here, looking at the park, up at the stars — Betelgeuse, Orion, the Big and Little Dipper. Roll down the window. Clink, the beer cans say when I throw them out. I have to be to work at 8. Starting the car.

Driving.

Stopping, I see they have it roped off. Everything's quiet. Gramma's specs pinch my ears. Three in the morning. It's been some night. Open the door, climb out. Reach in, look around. Get back to the trunk where a good bazooka's kept. She takes a 2.36 anti-tank rocket.

Throw down the chamois, kneel on the knee. Bazooka's ain't heavy. Hey, loaded up, that's me. Hey, sighting in, steady on the knee. Hey, 5th Street. Where are you? Marcus Sporting Goods. Tip-Top Tavern. 5th St. Hotel. Berger Hardware. —alvation Army. (Part's been burned off.) Outreach Mission and

Asembly Hall. Nummi Jewelers. —alvation Army. Hey, I let go. Hey, —alvation Hey, I'm mending. "Stop!" There's the screaming. Hey, bricks falling. I pack the bazooka. No Salvation. I drive off. The sound of war. Turn on 4th St., Baxter, Elm. Beany says, "Hello!"

Emma's Market

Fagerlin Fuel.

Broadmoor Manor

Beany says, "Hey, Good to see you again."

Phoenix Villa.

Leib's Place.

Jack, the Chili King's.

The Main Hotel.

Oh, Hanna, I'm not mending. The toilet seat fell on my head.

How are the electric trains? I drive the dirty air home past Q.T. and Tappa-Keg, taking the right turn at Ralph's Royale Market to the 4th St. tracks. I ride by the cafe with three names where she favored me once — Truckin' Inn. Derby Diner. High Bridge Cafe. I pull off Gramma's glasses. So dizzy coming home, Hanna.

Pulling in the lot. The apartment house. Lights are gone. All is still. My eyesight, now that I've returned the specs to my shirt pocket, is O.K. The dirty air ain't so bad now. Has she left me a note?

Inside in bed. No cops to bother me. Someone's asleep. His lights on. No note. Sleeping. I'm in my apartment sleeping.

Oh, God! How are they?

Oh, God! My trains.

Hey, Route of the Zephyrs, Bazooka love, and crazy old, dirty air, I hear her. Upstairs.

"Run that one again, Murray honey," she's saying.

"Sure, Baby," he answers.

"This time run it at this leg, straight for this leg, Murray." She's yelling it.

15 feet. O-gauge track. I hear the "Route of the Zephyrs" calling. I reach for my shirt. Pinch Gramma's glasses to my ears. Blurred stuffing, my torn heart lays in the corner. It's dizzy crazy and I've got the pain-grin, the pain-smile Walt Tessler knows. He's holding up the beams at work. All-white Walt.

Outside, I see the lights on upstairs, not mine. They're in the apartment upstairs. I open the trunk where bazooka love is kept. I hold you, my love, and everything's quiet at five in the morning. Everything but my trains. And Hanna. And Murray. My brains. My quiet.

I reach in, look around. 2.36 anti-tank rocket. Two left. The Maytag has suffered enough. I am inside the building and climbing the stairs. Throwing down the chamois, I kneel on one knee. "Open up, neighbor!" I yell, sighting in.

"Oh, God, Murray! It's *him*!"

"Don't worry about him, Baby, I'll turn up the sounds."

"God, we're having a good time!"

Hey, that's me being loaded up. Hey, sighting in, steady on the knee. Hey, Murray. Where are you? Hey, 5th St. Hotel. Tip-Top Tavern. Berger Hardware. Hey, —alvation. Hey, Murray. Gramma's specs make me dizzy. I look funny with them on. They pinch my forehead, and I can't see right. Hey, Hanna? Hey, Murray? True love Beany-Weenie's here.

Beany-Weenie shot the Maytag.

Hey! Back-blast. Look out!

Hey, bricks falling. Hey, Mrs. Kominski. Hey, that screaming....

THIS HEAT

WE COULDN'T HAVE SOMETHING LIKE *that* roaming the house. The first time we brought him in he gobbled up our bread and stew, our milk, butter, pies and doughnuts. Yes, gobbled us out of house and home. I disliked him for that. But oh, no! not my trusting husband Eustace who didn't call this fatty "junk" and "trash" until later.

Eustace, he would creep up behind him, whack him a good one on the seat of the pants, and disappear around the corner of the barn.

"W-h-u-t-s goin' on?" the fatty would ask.

"Why, Mr. Jack," Eustace would say, "right around here on the back o' your shirt it says, 'Kick me HARD!' Don't it?" HA-HA! Eustace would laugh.

He'd torment the fatty with a fake mouse he bought. He'd fill his shoes with a quart of preserves.

"Look-it how he don't know enough whether to laugh or cry," Eustace whispered to me that time the fat man slipped his feet into a pair of grape jelly brogans. HAR-HAR, Eustace howled.

He slapped Jack. He berated him for fun.

Now my husband Eustace is dead and Jack snuck off. He was to be our salvation. We bought him from the carnival to mind our store, but all he did was ruin our business. I used to see his fat and think, "God in your mercy put an end to this abomination," which Jack knew I was thinking because he'd turn to me and say, "You're lucky, Mrs. Sally." But lucky? For what am I lucky? Because Eustace died from a broken toilet seat and from the bite of a rubber spider? That's lucky?

Time after time, I used to yell at the fatty, "Stay out of the house. You've got room on your mattress on the porch." So what happens but home we'd come from Sunday worship and find a sugar cookie in the closet and tapioca on the bedspread.

"Well, let's think of a trick to cure him of all that eating," Eustace said when he was still alive. He had not yet been bitten by the vicious spider.

"Let's do him with a chicken," I said. And Eustace nodded. HE-HE! HAR-HAR! He knew what I meant. The sound of him was enough to get me going. WAH-HA-HA-HA! When I mentioned the chicken, he like to choked. "You sure we can afford another one?" Eustace asked.

We decided to try it on him next day. First we stole fatty's cap. Then we made him hold the chicken.

"Squeeze down and bite!"

"But ah c-a-n't, Eustace and Sally."

"You do as I say," Eustace ordered.

Jack sort of squealed. The chicken fluttered and pecked at his arms.

"Jack!" Eustace hollered.

"O-h-h-h!"

Blood came out when he bit down. We threw the squawking chicken away and gave Jack a big cigar Eustace had saved for this occasion. Jack was spitting chicken blood when we lit it.

BANG! The cee-gar blew up.

"Here's your cap back, Jolly Jack," Eustace said. HE-HE!

That scared him. We didn't try another trick till the eleventh day of the hottest month of the summer. That's when we did the one with the hands crawling up from the outhouse hole. Oh, my, Eustace, that Eustace! He's a funny one all right, a natural comedian!

"Here," he'd said to me, "feel of it."

"What you got there?"

"They ain't real. I bought fake ones where I got the mouse."

"Why Eust — HO-HO!" I couldn't say his name for the laughing that took hold of me.

"Come on out here, Sal," he said.

I got my cane, stepped around back where Jack used the outhouse. We have indoors plumbing — but not for the likes of Jack-Fat.

"Ha-Ha! He'll fall in," I said when Eustace showed how he was going to plant the rubber hands on the lip of the seat as if it were a body come crawling up from HELL.

"Here, let's me and you hide out tonight when he comes back from work."

We couldn't stop laughing. Eustace wanted to close up the fruitstand so we could get a laugh at Jack's expense right away.

"Don't let on nothing to him," I said.

At nine in the evening, we counted receipts and rolled up the awning the way we normally do. We helped Jack into the back of the pickup and drove home down the lane.

"G'night, Jolly Jack," we called, taking up a viewing perch inside the house.

He didn't go in right off, but dawdled around till near ten o'clock, then went to the outhouse.

"OH, HELP!" The door came flying open with a smash. Dust and splinters flew everywhere. Out shot Jolly Jack.

"HO-HO-HO! HA! There ain't no hands at all, but a pair of fake choppers clamped onto his be-hind. FAKE TEETH!" I screamed. "HAA! Eustace!"

"Joke's on me," I yelled a minute later when I almost died of fright.

So as to grab out at me, Eustace had put the fake rubber hands in the drawer where I keep cold creams and pin curlers —

After the chicken's blood, frightening, exploding cee-gars and false teeth in the outhouse, fatty two-by-four kept regular store hours like he was paid to do instead of coming into the house. Loudspeakers blaring, my fatty swatted flies or played with his flesh when we let him alone. "OH! MAN, IS HE FAT! MY MY! MY! HE'S SO FAT! IT TAKES TEN WOMEN TO HUG HIM AND A BOX CAR TO LUG HIM," the message on the loudspeaker would say. "HE'S A FAT, FAT MAN. WHAT YOU'VE ALL BEEN WAITING FOR! OH-OH-OH! MAN, HE'S FAT! HE'S LOADS OF FUN!!!" It was odd seeing him when you came down the overpass from the highway. His rear quarters draped over the couch, he'd sit in the lean-to (our fruitstand: we call it "THE GARDEN OF EATIN'") and sprinkle avocadoes with a watering can. He was so fat he was like one of those what you call "OR-A-CLES" and the grease dripped from his belly in that summer heat.

A month more of tricks and fatty got unkindness into his sour eyes. His nose sniffed out my wheat cakes. His mouth alarmed Eustace with the weak heart.

"I w-e-i-g-h seben hunnert and forty seben pounds," Jack'd say, then shake his belly, greasy ringlets of hair falling out from under his cap. "I eats light. Only thing stimulates me is the smell of frying hamburger. Seben hunnert and f-o-r-t-y seben. I'm thirty one. Size sixty two."

We made him spill root beer on his chin and neck when a person was watching. Even in sleep he wore a cap that said "Oklahoma City 89'ers." He wore it on his head like an umbrella from the tears of the world. A soiled T-shirt and raggedy coveralls made special at the Tent & Awning Store kept the rain off his shoulders. And his bare feet, they were always dirty. He was untidy about himself, downright unwholesome, you'd say. But the cars of the curious never stopped coming when the loudspeaker played, "OH, MY, COME IN AND SEE HIM, WON'T YOU, PLEASE? HE'S JOLLY JACK AND MAN HE'S FAT! A FAT, FAT MAN!" So we kept him on.

"Get up out of that bed!" I'd holler in the mornings. If he didn't move right off, I'd prod him with my cane. We made terrible fun of him every night of the week, *every* night, mind you. Sometimes I'd hear a sighing outside which was strong enough to move the living room shade where we sat a-laughing. Eustace said it wasn't but a gust of wind. Ol' trusting Eustace, I almost sent him investigating, but felt sorry. "My chest pains me, Sally. I need them heart pills again," he'd said.

We were up at ten the next day, and I remember Eustace's going out to the barnyard and checking the feeders in the hog lot. Later, among the melons, I could hear his muttering. He was bending over, grubbing in the dirt.

I grabbed my cane, walked outside. Eustace, given to them heart tremors, was standing in a patch of withered vines with no melons on them, not a one. He stood there tossing dust in the air, watching it fly away in the wind.

"Say, now, he's got a taste for watermelon."

We took the pick-up truck out to the lean-to fruitstand, the "Garden of Eatin.'" Jack was setting there waving to us as we pulled in. "Hi-dee," he called.

Real fast, Eustace took a fishing rod from out of the truck, cast a line and hooked Jack's cap right off his head.

"Now, Mr. Eustace and Mrs. Sally, please."

Eustace dangled it there in front of him.

"No sir. You want your cap back you quit the way you're behaving. You take another melon and you're a goner. Your big belly's gonna swell up. Why don't you just come to me and say, 'Please, Eustace, please can I have some melon?'"

Jolly Jack, a lump of suet and lard, scratched his neck and patted his toes. The fat man stared at my husband then produced a toothpick. He proceeded to work it up and down between his front teeth. "Lemme have my c-a-p."

Eustace lowered it. When the fatty two-by-four reached out, Eustace reeled it in. He did it again and again. Eustace was fishing.

"Sally, you better wake him with that cane of yours."

I did. I poked him in the chest and arms. He didn't seem to feel nothing. He showed his block-like teeth and began to chuckle. We had to examine the deep red mouth and the winding throat, just sit there and examine them until he began to shake his belly back and forth like we told him to when customers came to the Garden of Eatin.' He had them fake, false choppers on the counter. He started them biting. They rattled off the counter into the dust.

"You're trash. We know you been messing the house, too. Ain't he, Sal? Well, we got something called a pitchfork salad for fat fish."

Eustace and me were angry. It made us even madder when the fatty started in on his bottom teeth with the toothpick. Little, frail Eustace slugged Jack. He'd hit him before, but never like this. Which had no effect. My Eustace's arm and fist just flew out of Jack's big tummy. The fatty smiled, picked his teeth.

"You sleep here, you damn no good creature!"

Eustace cracked him on the forehead.

Next I knew, we were out in the barn with the herbicides and poisons. Sutan, Atrazine, Banvel and D-Con: Eustace was mixing them all. Treflan, Dyfonate. Horrible vapors arose.

"Fetch me a paper straw or a funnel," he yelled. In the garden, he carved a hole in a melon, a good, ripe one I hated to see go.

"Here now, Sally, grab a-hold here. Hold the funnel as I pour."

He pushed it in and poured out a poison drink for Jack.

"It ain't right yet," he said. Not all of the poison had made its way in. I've never seen him so angry as when he thought of that fat man. I figured Eustace to gulp down some of the poison himself he was so riled up. He took the melon and pulled out the funnel. He clutched at his heart as he rolled the wasted melon out into the dirt. Lifting a pitchfork, he held it in the sunlight. His arms dropped fast. The tines made a deep, clean wound in the melon.

"That fat boy's gotta pay. I'm gonna hide him a poisoned melon in the field tonight."

"Eustace, you got them pains? Are the pains troubling you?"

The next morning after Eustace had hid the melon in the patch, we went over to the fruitstand. Eustace got the gas can from out back of the truck.

Jack was picking his teeth. He didn't smile when we nodded to him.

"G'morning," we said. Drawing a circle with his boot heel, my Eustace tossed Jack's "Oklahoma 89'ers" cap in the center. Then he wet the crown and bill of the cap with gasoline.

"You're gonna have to answer for those melons, Jack."

"Why, Mr. Eustace, I feel sorta funny. I ate somethin' that didn't agree with me l-a-s-t night. I was so hungry and miserable and it looked so good. Yessir, and now my belly hurts."

The fire was going in a minute and Eustace added kindling to it. A black circle marked the place where Jack lost his cap.

"That poison shoulda took more hold," I said.

After the cap burned out, we asked that abomination of the Lord: "Feeling better?"

"Ah feels better, but Ah m-i-s-s my cap. Oh, here comes customers. Tidy?" he asked. Rubbing his hands across his face, he turned on the loudspeakers. He was drying his tears. OH, MY, COME IN AND SEE HIM, WON'T YOU, PLEASE? HE'S JOLLY JACK AND MAN HE'S FAT! He grabbed his belly and began to laugh and shake it about. He said it burned him fierce.

But a week later he was still there. "The poison ain't worked," I said.

"And he wants to come home!"

Eustace and me took precautions.

"Please, I need a bed tonight," Jack would plead. We'd made him sleep out back of the fruitstand.

"No, you gotta stay out here guarding the fruit," I would tell him. "But let's try on this here ol' necktie. I wanna buy you one to dress you up more for the people." I slipped one of Eustace's old ties around the fat boy's neck to get a better idea of how big a hangman's noose would have to be. (Back home, Eustace dangled a real rope from his hands as he awaited my measurements.)

"Wull, what you plannin' for me?" fatty asked.

"See to the customers," I said.

"Wull, when can I sleep inside the house?"

"You will."

"Wull, when? What you got in mind?"

"Soon."

It was hard putting him off. I didn't figure we could much longer. You can put up cement walls and haul out the artillery. You can tear down a fruitstand and even burn a cap. But you can't burn a road, and that's what he'd be coming down.

Then we heard him, HIM, heard him one night like a rumbling earthquake. It was early August when the noise of the storm came toward us from out close to the fruitstand.

"You hear it?"

Eustace and me felt the earth moving. We ran for the house. It was a good

58

thing.

"Ouch!" In a minute we heard the laughing fatty outside the window. "What you got g-r-o-w-i-n' out here? You see me yet? You up from bed? Am I wakin' you? Am Ah awake myself?" He was stepping on the nails and tacks we'd sprinkled in the yard.

"Get ready," Eustace whispered.

"E-u-s-t-a-c-e, Ah needs a place tonight. Please can I sleep indoors?"

Eustace was quietly lowering the rope. It dangled over the fat man's head who just stood there. "Ah w-a-n-n-a come in there, Eustace, please."

"GOT HIM!" Eustace hollered. "GOT HIM!"

We could see him struggling just below, hear his crying.

"Oh! What you doin'? I can't breathe with this necktie. You bought it too small."

"Quick," I said. "Lift. Hurry!"

We worked the handle, got him roped.

"SNAP!"

"Eustace!"

"BROKE! It done BROKE! He pulled it and it done BROKE!"

Down there we heard him. THUMP. THUMP. In the dark he must have fallen on some furniture. "E-U-S-T-A-C-E? Where're you now? And Sally?" He was whimpering. I swore the house was tilting.

"Hide yourself away," Eustace called.

"Oh, Lord. I can't stand thumping like that."

"It's them damn feet."

"Ah can hear you t-a-l-k-i-n,' Mrs. Sally. Eustace, will you see to my legs?"

He was slow. Thump, Stomp, Thump.

"We're goners."

His wheezing closer, he must have give in and set down. I woulda bopped him with my cane, Eustace punch him, but he stopped and sat a-breathin' outside. I could feel his air drafts through and under the door.

"Please, Mrs. Sally. Please, Mr. Eustace." He whimpered. He fumbled for the door. I held to my Eustace. Where we were hiding was in the shadows hoping he couldn't see us.

"Lemme in!" He was all out of breath. "I don't m-e-a-n no bother, but it's past m-i-d-n-i-g-h-t."

He was a catfish ... a bullfrog ... a carp!

"I'm seben hunnert and forty seben —"

CRACK! down came my cane. I hit him a lick on the head. He staggered back. "Now why'd you go and burn my c-a-p?" he cried. But in a minute, no more than a minute really, he passed. Like that he bumped and stomped his way down. He called after me once more, bumped around and was gone, air drafts and all....

We crouched there, heads together.

"What d'ya suppose?"

"He can't find his way out. He'll need our help for that."

"Don't you go down there, Eustace."

Then the house, where we lived for close to fifty-eight years, it began to tilt. Like a terrible, treacherous storm had hit it, we swayed up there, listening to him below where he must have been leaning on the walls again as he went from room to room doing Lord knows what damage. We heard the THUMP. STOMP. THUMP and the walls shiver and shake. Pictures rattled in the frames and smashed to the floor. My vases teetered and the rose lamp fell. Even Eustace's suit of Sunday clothes wiggled in the closet like it was dancing. I saw a crack in the wall which had never been there before.

"What can I do?" I asked Eustace.

It lasted an hour more. I peeked out to see an enormous hide, *Jack's* hide, making off for the woods beyond the melon patch. The moon wasn't out, but I could see him anyway.

We spent the night upstairs, fearful. We came down in the morning.

"Here now, sit on the sofa," I said to Eustace. "You take you a snooze and rest up." We were in the living room. "You can get up and have pie later. We'll give you a change of clothes and things'll be better."

He sat on the sofa. From the closet, I got him a bottle.

"Take you a good, long pull, Eustace."

He took a drink and lay his head down. "I think we're shut of him," I said. "I'll yell if he's around and we can quick run upstairs again."

I went out the screen door. I took a look around the farm buildings and seen the note on the clothes line. It said how we'd been awful good to him, but how he'd got to sleep inside somewheres else and so was leaving the farm. PS. I been drinking, it said.

"Eustace," I yelled, maybe a minute or two after I got in. "Eustace, oh, Lordy, no, someone's been usin' your milk glass." I also saw a cigar on the floor I'd missed earlier.

"I'm very weary," Eustace called. "Sally, I think I'm very tired from last night."

"Damn that fatty catfish," I said. I came in to Eustace with what was left of my blueberry pie. "Look-it what he done! The sink has a messful of dishes, and he gobbled us all out of food."

Eustace complained of arms and legs being weak, but he made it from chair to chair and into the kitchen.

"Look-it that fool. Look-it here what he left to scare us."

It was a can of peanut brittle from his carnival days. It said right on there TASTY PEANUT BRITTLE. HAVE A HANDFUL. When I unscrewed the top, out something flew. WHOOSH! A paper snake winding, grinning at us. It shot by and landed on the floor.

"Arhh," Eustace grabbed his chest and slumped a little forward. The snake scared him. It was a surprise to see it come flying out and around the kitchen.

"You come here with me," I said. I pulled him into the bathroom. There was a Bevo soda bottle on the floor. I showed him his toothbrush which had been

60

used by Jack-Fat. He put a match to it, melted it over the tub. "I don't want to see this toothbrush no more," he said.

"Sit down here," I told him, but caught him in time before he fell.

He took a long breath. Then he looked at the toilet seat where he'd almost sat. It appeared like he couldn't bring himself to do it at first.

"Go on ahead. You got to."

When he reached down for the seat, my worst suspicion was confirmed. It was cracked, falling apart. There was no lifting it.

"Oh, Lord, no, Eustace!"

"Looks like he didn't know his own strength," Eustace said. "Looks like he sat down here and didn't know his own strength."

He was breathing hard by then. His chest hurt.

"Get your pills from the kitchen cupboard if it's your heart. I'm busy here in the bathroom."

He held to the wall and sidestepped out. I heard him fall the next minute.

"Eustace!"

He was on the floor, just him and the paper snake. His pills were scattered around him.

"Sally, I got dizzy. What made me fall?"

"I don't know exactly, Eustace. Never mind."

"I sat down there, leaned over him and fed him his pills one by one.

That's when the vicious rubber spider attack occurred. Hung from a string, it dropped out of the ceiling, slow. I saw it, a rubber spider. I couldn't warn Eustace in time. His mouth full of pills, his heart cutting him the way it was, I just couldn't get the words out —

TRUE ADVENTURES

IN THE COUNTRY, SUMMER NIGHTS come on you in stages. I must have sat through these stages a hundred times the summer of the visitor. As the clock moved from eight-thirty to nine and beyond, it was like darker and darker curtains were falling over the corn and soybean fields that spread out from the house. I'd sit there watching the pumphouse, wheelbarrow, or rutting shed for half an hour and see no changes. Then twenty minutes later everything was darker. Then for awhile it was ok again until another curtain fell and another, until finally I could hear the 10:32 rattling by and Dory said it was time for bed.

In those days steam trains ordered our lives, mine and Dory's. I'm older now, but I remember my youth with the trains. In the morning the 8:45 went east to Decatur, the 10:17 west somewhere, the 1:05 east again. All through the day, they gave, they took away. Sweeping the fields at night, their headlamps found the farm and pried pale, snooping fingers into the yard or kitchen of the house where I sat in the darkness waiting. One minute the house would brighten in the headlamp's glow, and we'd hear the long, loud wail — Pa-a . . . Pa-a-a-a-a-a-a-a-a-a-s-s-s-s . . . Comin . . . Pa-a-a-a — and the next minute, the place would lay dark and quiet again. The steam trains taught us lessons. All hereabouts knew the lessons as we knew their schedules, the sound of their whistles, and what the whistles meant, like mine's saying, "Pa, Pa's comin'." Every farmer, wife and child knew the sound. Even the roses on the pumphouse wall took on a strange, beautiful light the moment the trains would shine on them. Roses in the night became beautiful in the glow. They were the same wildroses as clung to the pumphouse at noon, but now we saw them in a different light.

That one haunting, memorable summer of my first loss and gain the visitor came. He rode in on a freight from Morris or Coal City, out that way somewhere. Most drifters just kept on going past here, so I was surprised to see him throw out the wrecking tools and brushes and jump off. He'd been writing a company about putting their sign on country barns, he told us later. It would read, CHEW MAIL POUCH TOBACCO. TREAT YOURSELF TO THE VERY BEST.

"I've done rough, heavy, dirty work, son and ma'am, mostly railroad work," he said before Dory, my stepmother, hired him on.

It frightened me having him around when I wasn't used to seeing someone there. He had white hair. His face was red in places, the skin around his eyes blotched. Dory said, "Maybe his blood pressure's up and that's why it's that way." His eyes knew what trouble a body can get into. They saw right into you. About this, Dory said, "He's a worker who hasn't time for fooling with your likes. You

stay out of his way, Randy." I remember something else about him, how his nose
— not a very large nose — was sort of bent, or twisted to one side. It made his
face sad and kept him from catching his breath. Sometimes he'd have to sit
where it was cooler. Slumping forward under the tree, he'd heave his shoulders
with the effort it took him to breathe and wave us away. "I can't right now," he'd
say. "No air!" An old-timer, he could outwork me in the heat, however, whether
he could breathe or not. In fact, he could outwork me *and* Willie Horyza com-
bined, and Dory appreciated him for not spitting tobacco juice in the hired man's
house.

Soon after he came Dory let him know how little I did around the place.
Maybe that's why the barn had to go. Pa would've fixed it, but he wasn't here, and
we had to sell the livestock. We got a good, fair price. So now we didn't need a
barn. It was old, leaning and ready to fall anyway. Things'd been different if Pa
were alive. It hurt me talking of him, of how he'd died.

"Mr. Johnson, I expect you're wondering about my husband," Dory'd said
the evening he arrived.

The old boy nodded. Off across the farm fields you could hear a low rumble,
a banging of unloading and switching box cars.

"My husband ... his Pa," Dory said, "was a switchman on the C. B. & Q."

"I've rode it."

"My Pa was a good, honorable person, sir," I said.

"He was charitable to everyone who came by," Dory went on. "When
Randy and I returned one night from his Grandma's, we were stopped on the
tracks over by Arcola where the down-bound was being held up, red lights shining all over the place. I asked the conductor, who'd been out in the snow, 'What is
it?' 'Someone's suffered a heart attack running through the snow. Oh, Lord!' the
conductor said. 'It was too much running through the deep, wet snow that got
him.'

"That's how my Pa died," I said.

Dory said: "I cherish his memory. So does the boy. He loved his Pa, and I my
husband. He was forty-five when he went. This boy's had himself misfortune, I'd
say. His mother died when he was four."

She excused herself to work on some ironing before bed. "I'll see you two in
the morning," she said. Still feeling bad, I stayed out with the barn-wrecker.

"When I was your age I lost my own Dad," he said. "What was there left but
to leave my Ma and sisters and head out for work of some kind. I got a job working on the tracks for fifty-five dollars a month. When the sun rose over the rails
the corn burnt up, the pastures withered, and the cinchbugs controlled all. I'd see
farmers pouring oil around the fields to keep off rats and cinchbugs. It did no
good. Banks closed in town as the crops rotted. And what did I do but go swim-
ming in the river, diving deep under the current of the Wapsipinicon while these
good, hard-working farm people went under in other ways.

"I worked in a molasses factory a couple years, then on a barge. But I always
came back to the rails. Citizens of the country with diamond rings rode through

on passenger trains when I was young. I thought it-all was gonna be that way for me. I still ride the rails, but I'm as likely to share my Pullman with guys like Steam-Train Lucas, the Montana Clipper. Son, you know the town where I jumped off and into yours and your step-Ma's life?"

"Sure."

The barn-wrecker ran his hand through his hair and took a chew of Mail Pouch.

"When I was young in that town I saw the first streamline train I'd ever seen — the Queen of Gold. She stopped long enough to take water at the tower. Then off at 80 miles an hour. When she reached Denver, Colorado the news got back to us on the wire. I'll say she brought excitement ... 82 miles an hour all the way, 82 miles an hour of excitement."

The barn-wrecker told many a story that night. Dory'd already been in an hour.

"One time I had a spiteful fireman. When we pulled in to take water he overfilled the tank. Water ran down to where I crouched in the coal tender, and all trip long as the train swayed the waters washed back and forth. I was so wet and tired getting to Toledo, so wet and tired of being baptized, that I changed directions — as I would often in life. The next freight I caught went west. On it I fell asleep ... the next I knew I was on a railroad car ferry in Ludington, Michigan bound for Milwaukee. I woke up sailing in the middle of the lake. I'd gone from land to water without knowing."

"Did you ever pick up a nickname?" I asked. "You told me about The Montana Clipper, well ... did you ever have one?"

"My Pa's farm was near St. Peter — in Minnesota," he said. "That happens to be my first name too. What do you think I've been called for years now but 'Minnesota Pete' Johnson! That's enough talk for one night," he said and eased up out of his chair to the whistle of the 10:32 heading out into the mystery of the night. "That late already!" he exclaimed and snapped his pocket watch shut.

In my room, in the summer closeness upstairs, no breath of air stirred the curtains. I lay on the bed, the wet pillow behind me. Way across the fields I heard the last of the 10:32 and wondered whether Mr. Johnson heard it too and was planning his escape. But early next day, he was out there, as he always was, throwing down shingles from the rafters. I was to stack them in rows on the ground. Morning after morning, he'd clean up, then dry his face and hands with the hopsack hanging from the tree under which Dory sat evenings. He'd have a cup of coffee, maybe a piece of bread, then get to work. He'd climb the ladder, grab his crowbar, and another day had begun.

After an hour or two of hard work, he would climb down and talk awhile. "Did you ever hear of the Kiowa Indians?" he'd ask. Or he'd talk about some city he'd seen once and would like to return to some day. I never tired of his stories or his history.

"I was genuinely sick of railroading one time," he said. "I thought of staying around home. Then these fellas came by. What got me was they walked up, climbed a ladder standing beside the barn, then started to painting. With no guidelines, you drive a guy nuts.

"In the old time, it'd take me four hours. You don't outline or draw the words. You start with the 'P.' Eyeball in the rest." He caught his breath a minute before heading into the hired man's house. "Here," he said, returning a minute later, "we got us a wall left." We walked to the barn. Dory'd come out to hang wash. She watched from under the trees. With his fingers curled around a brush, he finished 'POU.' Then I began. He guided me on the 'CH.' That was the way to practice the CHEW MAIL POUCH sign—on a barn that was coming down whether you painted it right or not.

"I've said it to you before ... I've done dangerous work. No wheat in box cars is worth the effort anymore. This has all got a message, son," he told me. "People are worth risking something, even your life for, but not railroads." He put down his brush. I kept on painting as he talked. "I never once cared for things that truly mattered. I never cared much for honest people and wasn't one myself. I wanted only to line my pockets. But I should have cared."

Why was he telling *me?* Maybe I didn't work, but I'd been straight with Dory. He was almost kind of dreaming as he watched me paint the words TREAT YOURSELF on the barn. I liked to see him resting in the shade under the trees. It was mid-summer and too hot for him. He struggled to catch his breath. "Sometimes there's no air to breathe at all," he said. By that point, he was down to the rafters and was resting more often. Me sitting beside him, he'd tell how all those years he should've stayed on the farm in St. Peter instead of roaming around. But now in his old age he found a place he'd like to stay, and Dory didn't begrudge him anything. He was in no hurry these days.

"Go on and get those words started while I rest here another minute," he said. I was painting the Mail Pouch sign.

My brush still wet, I worked on T ... O ... THE, TO THE. He smiled, went on with his stories.

What I'm writing is like a toast, I thought. TO THE ... VERY BEST. I *was* making a toast. To a Grand Old Gent, I thought. To a fellow who has travelled around ... a man who has taught me lessons about true adventures and where to find them ... who has taken his time to help me and Dory ... and bring the world to us.

"I worked in railroad salvage where you clean out derailed or damaged freight cars for awhile. Had myself a little business," he was saying, "a one-man operation ... boss and helper both. If I met other crews out lookin' for work, I'd lie to 'em and send 'em off down a road so that I got to the train before them to set up shop, to lay my claim. This was all legal. The railroad signed us up to clean out the cars so they could get them back on the tracks. Sometimes when I was in a real pinch though, I didn't care and broke the law. If I was out of a job and real hungry, I'd do what I could to make a few dollars. Simple things like sweeping wheat. D'you know what I mean?"

"No sir."

"Sweeping wheat's like stealing it — from box cars. There's no way of justifying it. Getting older, I began to lose heart for that kind of activity. I wanted the honesty of a good man's life. I'd seen others defy their natural impulses to steal, lie and cheat when well they might have done those things. If these hobos could fight themselves down, I could too, I figured. After that whenever a crew came by and asked 'Where's the wreck we heard tell about?' I'd let them follow me to it. And after that whenever I was penniless and saw box cars with wheat left in them, I just walked on past."

Among other things, the barn-wrecker taught me how to jump off of trains, especially express trains, before you got in the yards. "Otherwise the railroad dicks get you." He also taught me the difference between bums and hobos.

Thus we passed a summer. As I tended the garden or stacked shingles, he tore down the barn and taught me these things. Even though I was afraid to climb up the ladder with him, me and the old guy were truly a couple of barn-wreckers.

Then August. I watched as he drew closer to the ground. From up near the sky, up near the peak and the barn's rafters, he worked down slowly to earth. The foundation the old barn stood on was solid like the barn-wrecker himself.

I went the opposite way, though. Seeing him up there so often, hearing his stories (sometimes if it was a real good one, he'd yell it down to me), well, such things made me want to test my courage. When some rotting boards and the stone foundation were left and the raspberries ripe and the corn ripening, I had an adventure with Willie Horyza. I'd always stayed behind before and was sorry I didn't this time. Willie told me I should bring a broom and meet him down by the tracks. We both crouched there when we heard the 1:07 come — all this after Mr. Johnson's talk of honesty. There must have been thirty box cars on the train. It squealed as it slowed to switch tracks, then stopped. Water dripped from the coal tender and steam hissed from the locomotive. Nobody could see us hiding. When the locomotive started moving again, the engine straining for all she was worth, Willie ran beside it, found an empty, climbed in, and pulled me in with him. In a minute he was sweeping wheat like crazy. They'd left a lot of it in this one.

He'd done it before. With my cap, I did as he told me and swept wheat into the sack. The cap got full of wheat. I realized then that I shouldn't be in there. I was sweating. Then the car made me lose my balance. I'd rather've been on top of our barn. But even that was part of the past. Hardly any barn was left when I'd gone to meet Willie that morning. The barn-wrecker, who'd lived so long in so many different places, was right now taking it away. "Sweep faster!" said Willie. "Get going!"

I hurried, swept as hard as I could. Willie'd sell the wheat or feed his Pa's chickens. He was no friend like Mr. Johnson. I trusted the old barn-wrecker; Willie Horyza I wasn't sure about. I couldn't find my legs as the train speeded up. We had three sacks and part of a fourth when he jumped out, but not me. I held to the inside of the rolling box car. It pitched and threw me about. Through the door, I saw track ballast and weeds and heard him yelling, "Jump! Jump!" But I couldn't. It was going too fast. I was frozen. We were speeding up the line. I heard the whistle — Pa-a-a-a-a-a . . . Pa-a-a-a-s-s-s . . . Comin . . . Pa! I shook and got sick. I hung on to my cap as the world rushed by outside. What'd become of Dory? I wondered. But at that moment, before it was too late, I remembered Minnesota Pete, an adventurer who'd seen the Queen of Gold. Then I thought of Dory and of how Pa would be ashamed to see me caught and dishonored.

Willie stood over me laughing. When he saw my head he stopped. It hurt me when I came to, and my hands hurt. I got sick. "C'mon, you gotta get home." He was almost crying. I had blood in my eyes. My head throbbed and beat. I'd got a big cut on it, Willie said. He couldn't look. "What you gonna do?" he asked. We ran. Willie told me to pull the cap down over my forehead when I got home. I was dizzy. I could make it alone, I said. I was all right.

My head hurt so bad when Willie left that I ran through the fields, holding my cap tight against the bleeding. I'd gouged my hand on a cinder. Part of the cinder was still in there. I'd hurt my leg, too, because now I felt it burning real bad against my overalls. When I thought of the train, the smoke, the banging, I got sick again and had to stop running. I felt closer to the barn-wrecker, though. We had something in common now. We'd done something great and daring. Getting to be like him wasn't easy. I didn't know if it was worth it after all. Still, if you wanted to be a man of the road, you had to do these things.

Dory almost fainted when I got home. She pulled me close and dragged me to the pump, and the barn-wrecker drew cold water. She dabbed the cut. She asked me what happened.

"I fell," I told her. "I cut my head on the concrete in town."

She got heated up and asked why nobody fixed streets and sidewalks. She washed my forehead, looked me over.

"That'll need stitches," the barn-wrecker said. "We'll get you to the Doc."

I wondered what he thought, whether he admired the cut and how I fought the pain. I wondered whether he'd ever seen such a cut. Then I put on the cap and some wheat fell out. I looked at Dory, who was rinsing a rag and hadn't seen. But Mr. Johnson had. Leaning against the tree where the hopsack hung, he'd seen the wheat fall out of my cap.

"Where'd you say you fell, son?"

Dory turned. Her eyes followed where he pointed his finger. When she looked at the wheat then at the barn-wrecker, I could see her face change.

He'd told on me, I thought. He'd told on me and gotten me in trouble. At first I didn't care how he felt, just about Dory. I looked at the wildroses on the barn and the pumphouse. They hung their prickly stems along the trellis. I looked at the wheat that'd fallen from my cap. I could see the barn-wrecker had been working. The barn was down. Except for the stone foundation, he'd pulled the barn down and I'd hardly helped that week. I was thirteen years old. He'd turned on me. How could he have? I kept thinking. I was crying — more because I lied and he'd caught me and told on me than because of any cut on the forehead. I cried, too, because of how we'd sold the hogs and torn down the barn. Dory and me were all alone now, the summer gone. I wondered what'd become of us if I kept on lying like that. It wasn't what happened to my forehead that made me cry so, or that I had no courage for barn-wrecking, sweeping wheat or stuff like that. It was everything else, everything on top of it — the sight of the hopsack, the painted sign, the wildroses on the pumphouse wall. I'd never cried like that before. I'd never felt so bad; for Dory, Mr. Johnson, myself. I sure don't know what got into me that time, nor how I'd ever see it right with them. On top of it all, I'd gone and sullied Pa's name.

But that was years ago. By summer's end, by the time the school buses started rolling down the farm roads looking to bring us all back in again, something in my life had changed. The barn I'd been afraid of climbing for so long was gone, and I was getting older.

"Son," I remember the barn-wrecker telling me, "I'll be leaving you and your step-Ma Dory soon, but I want you to know something. You became a workman over the summer. You became a man when it counted, son. I'm proud of how it turned out." He shook my hand, gave me a hug.

I believed him then, and I still do, though we never again heard from him. I guess I've always believed him because he was the barn-wrecker and never lied, not him, not Mr. Johnson with his wrecking tools and stories of the road. Once, in fact, when I was thirteen and wildroses wound up the pumphouse wall, he'd fixed *me* for lying.

THE KISSING BOOTH

I'M PEELOK PALM (DON'T LAUGH at a God-given name please!). I'm standing here in the crowd waiting for the curtain to open and the fool on stage to start explaining himself. He's Nate, my son-in-law. Beginning at noon, he goes every hour-on-the hour till nobody's left out here. For a dollar-a-head, you get to listen to his nuttiness then take a "tour of the grounds." Some tour! I come out here every afternoon in fake nose, glasses, and moustache to laugh at him. He still doesn't know it's Peelok behind the Groucho glasses. I even bring my grandkids in disguises. Think he recognizes them? The little one wears a Cinderalla outfit with an eyemask. But the boy dresses normally — a fake nose, fake glasses, and fake moustache similar to mine, but that's all. At two o'clock back goes the curtain and out steps their Daddy.

He's really something. Thirty people are here to watch. Here I am among the gawkers, a grandfather with two grandkids and he doesn't notice me, a man who has broken bread with him a hundred different times. He brings out a small table, places it on stage. He carries with him a woman's wig and purse, too. Then he signals the neighbor (a "basket-case" if I ever saw one, an old-timer, a widower who supplements his pension driving "the get-away vehicle" in Nate's clown show). So signalled, the neighbor starts up, circles the crowd and stage a few times in the pickup truck, then Nate takes hold of the mike and begins the show. Right away, I tell the kids to block their ears for a sec—

"Look yonder!" yells Nate the fool, pointing to the pickup truck circling past. Honking the horn, the neighbor pretends to wave good bye as he drives around. His arm is out the window. "It's the truck," Nate says, "where this whole cockeyed business started. It was her who began it with her wild talking as we drove back from the A&W last summer. And that's the truck where it happened. Look yonder, you tourists! Feast your eyes on it! See where the break up of a family began."

Nate's neighbor parks the pickup in the yard and heads for the stage. Knowing what's coming next, I bend down to the little ones.

"Keep your ears blocked just a minute longer, my honeys," I say.

"Sure, Grandpa Pee-lob," Mary-Kay says. She can't get it right. But how can you hold it against her? She looks up at me with those dreamy eyes that never seem to focus.

On stage, their father is yelling, "We were on the way home, I tell you, with my kids Sonny and Mary-Kay when May-bell started giving me a piece of her mind. I had to tell those goddammed kids, 'Shut up a minute so I can hear your

Ma!' "

I take the kids' fingers from their ears. "It's O.K. now," I tell them, "your Daddy didn't say anything bad against you." They smile at me through their masks. I say to them: "Here comes a part you haven't seen him do yet." (It's the good part, too, I think. I feel like telling them, if you really want to see your old man at his downright worst, this is it. That he could've thought up such a pathetic display!) The audience is howling as the neighbor, who has just got back from the truck, picks up the lady's wig and puts it on. The old fool stands there, a red, curly-haired wig on, hardly any teeth in his head, mimicking *my daughter* May-bell! Hands on his hips, he taps his foot, says to Nate: "Gimmicks! You've got to have gimmicks, Nate!"

This really gets the gawkers who surge close to the stage.

"Speak up or shut up, May-bell!" Nate yells into the mike at "my daughter."

"You've got to have gimmicks to make a roadside attraction work to interest people hereabouts." The neighbor starts curling the red wig with his fingers — an old man standing on stage with a wig on. Has he no shame? I'm furious to think anyone could portray May-bell this way. But I think on the bright side. It's worth it, I figure, seeing Nate act the fool.

"Gimmicks in reference to what?" Nate says. "You ain't referring to that giant, man-eating clam we saw in Livonia last summer! I hope not, woman. Don't you remember how we followed the signs forty miles to get there. Don't you think that was real ... that gurgling ... those bubbles ... the lighted eyes in the dark?"

The toothless, fool-neighbor digs in the purse, pretending not to hear him. (Oh my Good Lord! the thought hits me. It's Nate, these children's own father on that stage!) I feel a tug at my sleeve. The crowd of thirty is in stitches as they follow this little play-act, the neighbor mimicking my flesh-and-blood May-bell.

"What is it?" the little ones ask. They're curious. "Is it supposed to be our Ma?"

Nate has walked away to the edge of the stage now. It's hard believing he cannot recognize me or his kids. He's saying to all of us who've paid a buck to get in, "You tourists believe me. I didn't want to do it ... to slap her for sassing. But she kept diggin' at me."

"Nate," the bewigged neighbor calls, "how're you so sure about the clam? How close did you get to *really* seeing it?"

"How do you know I'm not sure what I saw?" he asks back.

"I asked you first."

They're both nuts. To go back and forth like that all summer — "I asked you first!" "No you didn't. I did!" — to go back and forth replaying the scene that led to the building of this rotten junk-heap Nate calls the "show." What the hell kind of place is this? What kind of stage? A couple of boards with some ragged, faded canvas thrown over them. What kind of actors? A broken-down, toothless pensioner whose pants are stained in front with Lord knows what, and a lunatic who thinks he's opened the Tickfaw Fine Arts Center. And here I stand with fake eyebrows, glasses, nose — the whole works. I've seen the "show" twelve times unnoticed. In the heat of the afternoon, I've perspired beneath the disguise, the fake plastic moustache tickling me, the nose hard to breathe through. What Sonny and Mary-Kay have watched so far are just preliminaries. It gets worse. Part of it I *do not* want them to see. "Get ready when I tell you to put your hands over your eyes. Don't let me catch you peeking, children," I say. "It's O.K. for you to watch now, but when I tell you not to —"

Nate's got a couple of boys in to help change the set while he and the neighbor are back of the curtain — what curtain? A couple of old, torn bedsheets running from the house to a tree? The stagehands bring out a mirror and place it on the table, then they carry in a kitchen chair and floor lamp which they plug into an extension cord and turn on. Everything set up, the hi-fi comes on. It's a slow, jazzy tune coming from backstage. To show you how stupid my — how I hate the words — son-in-law is, here we're all of us beneath the hot afternoon sun and he's got on a light for the famous "seduction" scene.

"Close your eyes," I tell the kids when the neighbor comes out. He's still got on May-bell's red wig. But what's worse, now the old, boney pensioner is wearing her ... bathrobe! Nate's nowhere to be seen. The sight of the neighbor dressed like that gets the audience roaring. They're pointing at him, the men whistling. Out to midstage comes the neighbor, bathrobe, wig and all. Plunked down in the chair, he starts examining his face in the mirror. He scrapes his hands over his jaw, looks closer. "I need a shave," he says. The crowd titters. A fat guy in front laughs and chokes.

"Nate, honey," the neighbor hollers back at the curtain. "All I'm saying is any place you've ever dragged me the past five summers has had a gimmick to make it work, to make it stick in people's minds. Every last one, Nate. How about that horse frozen in Lake Shirley? Why that was no more a prehistoric mammal than little Mary-Kay, our daughter, with her, her —"

"Shut up about them eyes!" I hear Nate yelling from behind the curtain.

(Mary-Kay's had Bell's Palsy and her eyes are crossed just a little. Nate never liked to catch anyone laughing at her.)

"Is he talking about me, Grandpa?" Mary-Kay asks.

"No, honey," I say as the neighbor starts in again up on stage.

"... then that Burt Higgins, the so-called 'ecty-morph.' Remember how they advertised him when all he turned out to be was a sick old man in need of a kidney operation? That stuff's got failure written on it. You're asking for trouble when you can't keep promises to the paying public. Now if a man had brains, he'd advertise a mystery show."

Out pops Nate right then — in the goofiest thing, his pajamas and slippers. "Mystery show?" he asks.

"Oh," says the neighbor being coy, "I guess I'm ready for bed."

"No, wait ... about this here show."

Then the neighbor does something most anyone would find repulsive. What kind of idiot stoops to these things? O.K., he can't get by on social security and needs a few dollars. But is this the way? Up around his knees, he pulls the robe. The crowd gasps. They notice the nylons. Like roadmaps across the whiteness of his legs, you see the blue varicose veins as he rolls the nylons down his legs.

"Shut your eyes quick, you kids!" I tell Sonny and his sister.

The crowd is hooting and whistling and Nate yelling, "Tell me about a 'mystery show.' What do you mean by that phrase?"

But why stay to hear such crazy things when the kids are getting hungry and fidgety.

"Here," I say through my mask, "Grandpa will fetch you something to drink, maybe a hot dog or something, too. How's that?"

"Thank you, Grandpa Pee-lob."

I take their hands. Together we wind our way through the crowd out back. Nate's right at the edge of the stage loud-talking into the mike. "I'll tell you what, you people," he's saying, "when she said that about its being a mystery, I thought to myself how, if I played my cards right, I could have signs made up and I could use my truck to advertise. When I saw all those signs flying off my workbench with ???A BAFFLING MYSTERY??? and DO NOT WAIT ANOTHER MINUTE! and ???WHAT IS IT??? written on them, I don't mind admitting, I reached over and right there give her a big kiss, which on account of my whiskers she don't ordinarily allow."

"Now I got whiskers, too," Gabby says. I turn to see him rubbing his chin, the wig fallen slightly forward. The old fool!

Mary-Kay and Sonny order the dogs from one of the stagehands who operates concessions.

"Can you eat that with your fake moustache and nose?" I ask Sonny. He nods, takes a bite. The black plastic moustache and the nose move up and down with each bite. I have a Coke.

Always the curious one, Mary-Kay asks, "What's Daddy saying?"

"Just how he got this place started before you, Sonny, and your Ma left."

"He had me walking downtown with a sandwich board," Sonny says.

"And your Ma had to ride around in the truck advertising the 'gala event' out back of the Nate Greeley's place. It was going to be a 'mystery spot,' he said. Remember, kids, how your Ma had to talk through that bullhorn all day long?"

"I came up with the first mystery item, too, Grandpa Pee," Sonny says. "A very old, mysterious silver tooth."

"Your Dad's a fool, son. Do you know that?"

"Yeah, I guess I do," he says slowly, sadly.

I buy him ice cream to pick up his spirits.

"Don't get it on your moustache," I say.

When we head back, we hear Nate so excited he's almost crying, almost sobbing telling about the junk he was rounding up. The neighbor's gone from the stage.

"My old barn's not so big, as you see," Nate says, pointing to it over beyond.

"Well, back then it was filled with old Packard engines, third-hand baby carriages, and such like. You can imagine the problems I had getting it all cleared out. But one rainy Saturday, Gabby and me rolled up our sleeves and cleaned her out good. My boy Sonny discovered the first satisfying item. You had to look hard to figure it was a tooth. What I couldn't get out of my head as a mystery for the show was Happy's tumor, that's Gabby's dead wife, preserved in alcohol and setting in their kitchen cupboard all those years."

At this the crowd gives out a laugh. "How'd he get the old lady in the cupboard?" someone yells.

"Quiet down now," Nate yells back. He's crying with emotion, actually crying tears down his face. "I made up my mind to put out any other fine curiosities that came along for public display," he's saying. "That is until we got home. Fixin' for bed, my old woman May-bell ('I guess I shoulda put *her* in the cupboard with Happy!' Nate says and laughs) my old woman May-bell, who'd been sulking all the way back from the A&W, started in complaining." Nate stops, looks back at the curtain, clears his throat. "My old woman May-bell, who'd been sulking all the way back from the A&W, started in com-PLAINING!" He yells it, and this time the neighbor hears and sticks his head out. "No kid of mine is going to become a spectacle for every fool with a quarter in his pocket to burn," he says, mimicking my daughter.

Then Nate goes on. "Let me tell you tourists: Listen to your old woman and you'll get where I almost got — nowhere! But I had sense *not* to listen. Them kids did as I told them. Sonny, he carried nails and boards around when I asked. Mary-Kay cleaned up the yard. And if that witch-woman nagged at us, I tore after her into the house. From then on, I can't even start to telling how the thing went up. But just look at that barn! I hammered and sawed and built me a Taja-Mahal. I sent Sonny out around town putting up signs advertising the ?mystery spot? while May-bell simmered in the house, afraid to come out.

"So she didn't dare hinder me anymore, and I went along fixing the place, building booth after booth of mysteries. The place was getting to look more and more like a show every day. Outside, I spiked an old sheet over the barn door with a question mark and an arrow saying: ?THIS IS THE ENTRANCE↓ and inside I had crepe hanging from the rafters and a sawdust floor to walk on and rose colored lights blinking. All along the walls were mystery booths out of peach crates. And at the end, at the exit place, was the Kissing Booth where she'd sell kisses for .25¢ on the dollar, if I had my way. It was just a little stand with a counter you could lean over. 'Quarter a Kiss,' the sign would read. 'Kiss me, Honey!' ... Twenty-Five Cents.'

"Well, I guess I didn't understand her. That's always been my problem. See, May-bell, who sat there watching all those days as I was fixing things right, well, she finally denied me and my show just as we were fixin' to open it, ? 'THE ROYAL MYSTERY SHOW' ? I even had a United States flag on the barn roof and a loudspeaker playing music and my new gabardines on. That's when she refused and wouldn't change for nothing. When she gathered them kids around her I suddenly thought how it would of been better had they not been born at all. But it don't do no good cursing. I could see she wouldn't be persuaded, so I sneaked out to the barn and put another record on the loudspeaker. Then I got ready for the crowds and to count my money.

"Maybe I shouldn't of done her that way, I thought after a while. Sometimes, I don't know, I start to shaking and think I'm gonna pass out I get so confused upstairs in the head. Anyway, I no sooner got out there but she comes after me and sails a brick right over my ears. It hits the hi-fi and the whole thing collapses, Ker-Plunk. Then she starts crying and threatens to take away them kids and shoot me in the forehead if I embarrass her anymore. I remember to this day what she said: 'You're a bigger fool than I mistook you for, Nate. Tomorrow I am gonna see Rev. Carter and Dr. Hibbs about you. In the meantime, don't try to find me and the kids, as I know you will! There's hamburger in the freezer. Thaw it, but don't try to find me!'

"That and every evening afterwards were heart-breaking — looking over the hanging gardens of crepe and drooping flags in my own backyard. In fact, I like to took to drink if it weren't for Gabby who'd come over from next door every night and talk. On those summer nights, my kitchen never seemed so small. I couldn't breathe in there. From now on, May-bell and her old man Peelok Palm could stay clear of me because I had no use for either. You people out there, you tourists, hear me out! May-bell puts on airs. She thinks she's better than anyone. She gets it from that old Peelok who has seniority at the lumber yard and don't no more have to load trucks or saw boards. I have news for him, too, and that is: you'd better not come here to the Royal Mystery Show, Peelok, if you're so almighty careful of your manicure. I'm a man not afraid of work like *some* people I know.

"Well, if there's one thing I learned, it's that in summertime when you got a show to open there's no time for laying around the house feeling sorry for your life. One day, in fact, May-bell even came back to spy on me. When she saw I still meant business and that I was going about sprucing up things, making signs, and raking and planting, she set in to threatening again. She made as if to call the sheriff. 'You'll be put in the asylum yet,' she said. But when she saw I wasn't listening, out she flew on her broomstick.

"All I know is I'm going through with it. I've built something in the barnyard and barn she couldn't do in one million years. And how I see it is in another year or two, I'll have a valuable wild animal collection, a ferris wheel and maybe some bumper cars. And over there will be a souvenir shop and miniature rayroad with unusual ?mystery? items on display for sale. And if she was so damned smart-alecky driving off to her Daddy's with those kids last summer, what I want to know is this: what has she, May-bell Palm, daughter of Peelok Palm, ever done with *her* life? Now if you will all step over to the barn."

He jumps down and the thirty gawkers who've paid their dollars follow. Me and the kids trail along. Nate pulls open the barn door where we enter under the white sheet with the arrow and sign. It's pretty dark inside. You can hear slow, jazzy music again from a hi-fi Nate gets going. The old barn has a combination fertilizer, gas and oil smell. Thirteen times now I've been in that show and out of the afternoon sun.

"Don't you be frightened, Mary-Kay," I say. I thought I heard her whimpering. "Sonny-boy, you stay close by. Fix your disguises both of you."

"Yes, Grandpa," she says. The other one takes my hand. No matter how often I've come here to the darkness, the place amazes me. Where was Nate when they passed out brains? It gets me, the sheer stupidity! He's got little "displays" set up down the walls and in the center of the floor. They're on tables, some decorated with crepe paper streamers. Everytime I enter the loony-bin, I think, this guy's really nuts. So why do I bother?

"Grandpa Pee, here's my booth," Sonny calls.

"Shhh!" I tell him. We look at it, an odd, little tooth in a bed of — get this! — lettuce! What the hell? It doesn't make sense, I think, nothing here makes sense. Is it Modern Art? Do we have some kind of genius on our hands here in Tickfaw? The booths are mostly peach crates you look in. On the front they've all got painted question marks (?) you look at, as though somebody in his right mind would care what junk's inside. This one before me I've heard about from May-bell: a corn severed from his step-sister's twisted foot, Bertha was her name; next to that another peach crate "mystery," three agates and a gallstone inside a colored bottle. It takes no genius to figure that one out. Sonny and Mary-Kay beside me, we side-step booth to booth, each crazier than the next. Booth ?5? — a parched and faded snakeskin with the mysterious letters, a, q, b, printed down its back; Peach Crate Booth Number ?10? — two radio tubes and a heating grid from an electric toaster, all made to light up and glow when the booth is pitch black; Peach Crate Mystery Booth ?17? — rake tines sticking up out of a sawdust pile with some kind of dead worms weaving around and through. That's real artistry! There are ?29? others awaiting, and I am exhausted already.

Nate has kind of a chute to guide you through them all to the exit.

"Hurry, Grandpa," the kids yell. I fix my disguise and follow, getting angrier by the minute — not at the little ones, mind you, but that ignoramus. People laugh and point at displays. Sometimes, as at Mystery Booth ?23? — a marmot Nate caught and mounted and dyed turqoise for the show — they hold hands to their mouths. "Ooooh!" they say in sheer appreciation of its beauty. Later, at the exit they crowd around before leaving. It's hard telling why. Each time before, I've just walked out the door, but he must've added something or got someone to staff the kissing booth.

When we get closer, of all things I see that fool Gabby. He's got May-bell's wig and bathrobe on, lipstick smeared over his mouth. People chuck quarters at him as they pass out the exit. I laugh when I see what he's got written on the booth: ".25¢ *NOT* to kiss Gabby!" Oh, Lord, it's par for the course, I think.

"Grandpa," the kids are saying. "Look-it who's here." They're pulling my hands to go see. .25¢? Gladly! I think. We get up there and I toss him my quarter "exit fee." Already the afternoon's cost me for admission, snacks, now this.

"Hold on there," says the old, social security pensioner. He shows me the toothless smile close up. The red-painted mouth sneers at me as he kind of primps his hair. "Kids count too!" he says. "You can't cheat Gabby."

He hasn't recognized us. I straighten my disguise, reach in my pocket. Nothing! There's nothing there! "Kids count too," he cackles. He's so old his hand shakes as he holds it out. Other people are laughing at us now, and Mary-Kay and Sonny start that whimpering.

"They count like hell!" I say, starting for the exit. But his boney fingers grab my shirt and pull me back momentarily.

"Lady," I say, "if you'll take your hands off me and loan me your lipstick, I'll either pay you or kiss you to let us go."

"Sure," he says, "on-y you gotta pay for them two honeys."

He hands me the lipstick with which I draw two lips on my knuckles.

"Here!" I say. "Kiss this!!!" I let him have it. "And give me back May-bell's bathrobe!" The kids are yelling and clapping. When he falls the booth comes down around him. I jump in on top and start to unbutton the bathrobe. When I see what's happened, I jump back. "Oh, my God! BUCK NAKED!" I yell. Except for the black nylons, he's Buck Naked where the robe falls away. I see his old, white, wrinkled skin. Then from the corner of the barn comes Nate. He grabs me, pulls off the fake glasses and nose. He does the same to the kids' disguises.

"Peelok Palm! I might of known. What do you mean trying to sneak out like that? And bringin' my kids in here," he says kind of crazy-like. "Cover your eyes from the sight of woman!"

The old man is moaning in the heap the kissing booth has made. The sign "Kiss me, Honey" has fallen over his parts. I reach for the lipstick, paint my knuckles red again. Freshened up, I kiss the proprietor once, twice on the cheek and then once on the nose with my fist. He grabs me and shakes my shirt a minute, then gives up and tumbles on top of the old geezer. This done, I quick grab my disguise and my grandkids and herd them through the door.

"Kissing booths you have to pay to get past! Whew," I tell them, "that's enough Modern Art for one day!"

79

STAN AND OLLIE

OLIVER GETS UP FROM THE BED. He tries to hold her but trips over the piano stool in the middle of the tiny room.

"It's easy for you to go away just like that without seeing me!" his wife Cha-Cha says. She wipes her face on the wedding smock she's put on. "I sit here in the heat and never hear a thing. Sometimes I wonder if you'll call. It's like I'm para-lyzed. I can't move. It's like cinchbugs got me."

He has parked the truck, the big rig, up on the hill. "Do you have to bring it back now?" she asks. "You got here, now you're going."

"I'll be back," he says.

In the heat, the moustache tickles his face. The dust his boots kick up bothers his emphysema. He crawls up into the diesel cab. On each dark, metallic-blue door with its chrome handle, he has Stan's and his names painted, "Stan & Ollie, Mayville, Montana," then two bowler hats tipped so the brims touch. He listens to the engines. He pictures Cha-Cha standing on the porch, gazing at the sun. Burn it out of her, he thinks, burn it out of her good! During the last month, he's put as much country between them as possible. But in the end who does it hurt more? he asks himself. Leaving her alone is like an open invitation to the valley. Who'd want to haul a load over to South Dakota, Nebraska and Iowa and leave such a pretty thing by herself? Stan Laurence sure wouldn't, and *hasn't*, thinks Oliver. Stan wishes to stay home all of the time now, watching T.V. or ... well ... visiting Mrs. Hardesty. The last trip out, as Cha-Cha Hardesty sunned herself by the creek, he, Oliver, sweated and cursed his lot in motels from Spear-fish to Sioux City. He'd tried telephoning. No answer. He sent a post card. "SICK," it said. "SICK OF HIGHWAY. SICK OF SOUTH DAKOTA. HOW'RE YOU?"

He shifts gears, brings the big rig to a halt. He jumps down into the parking lot. His neighbor and partner is inside.

"Hello, Stan," Ollie says.

His partner isn't happy to see him back. Stan has the look he gets when he's been drinking. He can mimic the comedian Stan Laurel. He's mastered the fluffed-up hair, the long, v-shaped smile.

"Hello, Ollie. You were out a long time."

Ollie takes a beer. "It was hot. I broke down a couple times outside Sioux Falls. When you going to take a run yourself? Ain't we partners?"

"I've been thinking about it," Stan says. "But I like it too much at home. When you're gone out on the road I get to hear your phone ring across the valley.

I hear it way over to my place. Cha-Cha's never home, eh? No answer? I haven't seen her."

"What do you mean she's never home? She's waiting for me right now," Ollie says. "But I'm in no hurry. That's right, maybe I'll stay here awhile." He enjoys the beer, the bar fan's sigh. "I guess I had her figured wrong."

"So who says she's out home?" he asks his partner. He has a way of getting under Ollie's skin. To make it worse, he scratches his head, smiles with his mouth curved up.

Stan's questions startle Ollie. It's something to think about. Suppose she's skipping out on me right now, Ollie thinks. But hasn't she promised me later in the dark something meant for men and women, for Ollie and Cha-Cha? "What business is it of yours, Stanley?" he asks.

Oliver likes Tommy and Lena's Cafe. They have a good catfish platter. The men here are hard workers, he thinks — farmers, truckers. It's a comfortable place. Calming down, he does his Oliver Hardy routine. He does it out of spite. Mr. Hardesty imitates Mr. Hardy to spite and hurt himself and make himself feel worse. He has a bowler hat on. Stan's wearing his, too. "Why don't you do something to help me, Stanley?" he asks. Where the comedian would flutter his tie, Oliver uses the front of his shirt.

He excuses himself. Buying Stan a beer, he walks out to check something in the truck, then starts down the road. It will be quieter this way. I'll leave the rig for Stan. It ain't so far that I need a ride, but I certainly can have one with any of the guys. I sure know them well and can have a lift, he thinks. This ain't so far that I can't leave the cab and walk it in silence and peace.

He does the Oliver Hardy again by himself in the middle of the road. Dreaming of Cha-Cha Hardesty, he lifts the bowler, flutters the shirt front, whistles the cockeyed tune. He hurries over the pavement, hurries as fast as his legs and heavy frame will go. In places weeds grow through the concrete. Across the fields, dust rises from the flat, dull, burnt-over countryside. She's lucky having the creek even though it's dried up through most of the summer. He thinks how sometimes she sits out and lets the sun turn her golden. She's uncommonly beautiful, he thinks. Will the creek dry up again this summer? Will she be sunbathing beside it as it trickles its last and runs out? And will his neighbor and partner Stan be beside *her* as good ol' Ollie guides the big rig through North Platte, Yankton and places unknown? The crazy, cockeyed tune runs through his head, Stan and Ollie's theme.

Out of nowhere comes Swenson's bull loping along in easy strides over the brittle pasture, so that actually Oliver doesn't know when he's begun to speed up, as he's seen Stan and Ollie do in "Sons of the Desert," but it is as if he's trying to outpace the bull, the creature keeping up with him step for step, halting when he halts, charging in again, a huge leathery thing on the other side of a fence, snorting, shaking its head immoderately as if it has heard rumors about Cha-Cha and Stanley. Now Oliver is running full force, his mind full of Cha-Cha, the bull plodding onward all the time, its great bulk distressing him. As the bull outruns him, it seems to Oliver that it outwits him as well. He strives to keep abreast of it, only to fall farther behind, and the locusts' screech deafens him. He has to clamp his fists to his ears — the rumors. Around him their shrieking grows loud so that it is difficult to think until up ahead he spies the end of the fence, the bull veering off in search of something on the other side of the field. "I'm coming, Cha-Cha Baby-Honey!" he hollers.

He thinks of Stan scratching his head, giving him the Stan Laurel smile. He thinks of the fine mess Stan has gotten them into this time.

In the valley below are the house, the white bridge, the creek. No one's down there, he thinks. His breath comes hard. "If she's only at the well, I'll be happy," he says to himself. He runs into the kitchen, wiping his flushed, angry face. Why doesn't she answer? he wonders.

He hears locusts screeching. It is no cooler in the living room. Confused, he runs headlong through the hallway to the stairs, ripping down the curtains. God, how his head pounds! It feels as though something's in there behind my eyes, he thinks. Once before it'd hurt like that, once when Cha-Cha hurried past him as if getting back to the farmhouse before him could have saved her. It was crazy. When she got home she actually denied being out. Yet with his own eyes, he'd seen her in the August twilight. He'd even stopped her on the hill. But right to his face a few minutes later, she denied it. She even denied that he'd spoken her name and looked into her eyes as she, his wife, Cha-Cha Hardesty, had slapped his face. "Fool!" she'd seethed. She'd spit out the word and right to his face later denied saying it, slapping him, or ever going out at all. She denied it when every star in the heavens, even the new moon looked down.

"This time I won't believe her denial," he mutters. "I won't wait for her to come home."

No, this time, he thinks, bursting out of the back door, running with renewed and violent effort in the direction of his neighbor's and partner's farmhouse on the hill, this time, no longer loyal to the Sons of the Desert, Mr. Hardesty will interfere with Mr. Laurence, who is already interfering with Mrs. Hardesty.

I, LILLIAN

"Before you leave, let me take your photo for the keepsake album," I beg the boy. He agrees, and in the view-finder of the box camera, I center the stone chimney and the river. I so dearly want photographs — not simply of the house and frozen river out back, but of how it was before Big Sammy turned against me and the boy, threatening to return in the middle of the Minnesota night and do us harm. The boy is heading south to Beaver Bay the way the rest of them have gone. He'll leave me in the woods with my husband; at the very mercy of the winds that drift the snow before the door. Before that, however, I want the boy Arvid's photo.

He was only a recent arrival. His first time here he had a cup of chocolate then slipped off to the guest rooms in the attic to play "Johann Pa Snippen." The longer he stayed — two days the first time, a week the second, a month the third time — the better he got along with the wayward girls of the Blue Rondo. He seemed particularly attracted to one. Signe was by no means pretty, yet, out of all of them, she got him up dancing. While other, prettier women failed with songs struck from banjos or mandolins, Signe kept him twirling and spinning till bedtime.

There was an odd thing about the boy, this winter dreamer, however. When his dancing was over, how in heaven's name could Signe ever take him to her bed if he was forever tuning his ebony flute? When Signe was with him, she was so happy I could see her losing track of the days. But he was aware only of his music, which he rarely stopped. His broad, healthy shoulders, ripe lips, and blue eyes were too precious for other women, Signe felt. She knew that like his dreams, these assets had to be guarded, kept from the others who were so vicious. She knew he needed someone sensitive and attentive like her. But that flute he carried with him! It seemed to get in the way.

I, Lillian, often viewed him as he crouched near the ice caves. He would borrow my box camera, watch Signe like a wolf, and snap her photo when she wasn't looking. By then the other women knew he'd found her bracelets and wire earrings in a hideaway by the shore. He'd spy on Signe and steal her trinkets from a box she kept hidden in the ice. But face to face later, he was simply an honest wanderer who played the flute. From the day they learned of his thieving, all the fallen women in the place, old and young alike, vowed to help Signe deflower him. A thief is free to come up here, but a chaste thief, no! When Big Sammy and some of the camp-hangers-on caught him wearing Signe's trinkets beneath his sweater, some of them wagered on how long it would take her to make him a man, on how long it would take Signe Linnea to get at him.

"He won't be a boy in seven more days," they said.

"Fewer than that!"

"He won't last out the night. He'll be hers by midnight."

Betting fever had the place in an uproar. What else is there to do up here when the cold sets in? In the Blue Rondo we will bet on anything — the size of Signe's breasts; who can walk farthest on snowshoes; how cold it gets May twenty-first. While I had the chance, I should have taken him on myself, shown him *my* secret spots just as any woman would. But Big Sammy had something up his sleeve and said nothing to all this. That's how the trouble began: Sammy promised to bring someone else in to help with the seduction of the thief. I did not hate Sammy then, not as much as I would come to.

"Do you remember Marcella DuBois?" he had asked me.

"Yes. Didn't she have nine toes?" I said.

"She's an old woman who sleeps in her skirts by the fire. Last summer's moss hangs to her coattails," Sammy said. "I saw her on the road to Temperance River where she was bringing a musical show to the logging camp. I saw her west of the beech tree. She'd gotten her cart stuck in the river ice."

He'd asked her here, I found. To repay a favor, he'd invited Marcella to the House of the Blue Rondo to make some money. And because she and the boy on whom Sammy wanted to bet were musically inclined — the boy with the ebony flute, she with the gypsy fiddle — Sammy hoped that they'd appreciate each other. He wanted Marcella DuBois' confidence. He'd pay her for it. He petitioned the Lord and Marcella to know the moment at which the boy fell victim to Signe's flesh. For if Sammy had this information and no one else but Marcella (and Signe, of course, who was the victim of it all), then there was no telling how much my husband could win betting on winter evenings. Such is the power of music!

The old hag, you see, would be a sort of insurance, a *confidant*. She could provide Sammy facts about Signe and the boy which none of the others would, or could know. Because he's a tyrant, Sammy should never lose a bet. When he's happy we're happy, but cross him and he'll hurt you. The few times he's had to make good on a gambling debt, the Blue Rondo shook with his rage. A huge man with tufts of red hair on knuckles and head, I've seen him raise an axe and seven strokes later have firewood for an evening. Once, he slapped me so hard my ears rang three days straight. Another time he made me strap a catalogue to my chest so that he could fire (yes, believe me!), so that he could fire his .22 at the words MONTGOMERY WARD 1928. His bullets lodged in "Men's Underwear." I prayed that the new visitor was the answer and Godmother to all his fortunes.

So one night she came, the old lady, arriving in the middle of a storm. She shook the chill from her bones, and Sammy nursed her with drinks, soup, and bread. Then she pursed her lips and to her chin hugged the fiddle. I was certain the boy had never seen such a spectacle. I swore he'd burst for joy. He tried his flute. He pressed close to listen and clapped his hands while the girls about him whooped and sang.

Sometimes peculiar affections grow rapidly deep in the woods. The flute player was enamored of the old lady who'd come in from the storm. He was so given over to her that the following morning he wasn't happy until he should hear something from Marcella DuBois' fiddle. All day he was entranced by her music. And recalling what Sammy had asked (Sammy *demanded*! He *never* asked), Marcella directed the boy's attention to Signe as she washed her hair or, naked, cut butterfly strokes through the steam in the bath. There, that's the one for you, she said and pointed to Signe. "Go on there and give her a kiss, Mr. Flautist!" Then she would whisper to my red-haired husband, "I have the facts on them. I know it won't be long now and they'll be —" She stopped there to make a gesture with her fingers.

Big Sammy was never happier than when it looked as though he'd won. "It's clear," he said, "in one night this celebrated fiddler has bewitched the boy!" Sammy bragged about how what everyone in the camp waited for — the boy's entrance into manhood with Signe Linnea Siggurdson — was mere formality. Now he went slapping his men on the back as they ate sausages, cheese, and coarse, dark breads. But, I, Lillian, keeper of the Blue Rondo, he bullied because I didn't share his joy. What could I do against a man so powerful? I hated Big Sammy who fed me dry bread and coffee if I was lucky, then pushed me into the corner when the musicians' music filled his crazy head.

But one night through the frosted window I saw the boy with a light in his hand staring at me. He tapped twice, signalled and held a rain slicker and a bear-skin around me as we walked through the terrible cold to a place outside the Blue Rondo. On the way, I let him put his fingers around my arm. He did this so gently. He reassured me. I let him touch my ears. The tenderness he showed me, a woman of forty, is seldom seen up here. Then we were out of the snow and the wind.

"Will you sit with me awhile in the dry straw?" he whispered. He had to draw me to him, I was trembling so. He helped me with my overcoat and covered me with straw.

Next morning, Sammy found me peacefully asleep. He shook me with his horrible red fists. He questioned me. I pretended not to know what he was up to.

"I came in here alone."

"You don't wear work boots, Lillian. Whose tracks are those in the snow outside the door?"

He paced the floor, bull-like, flexing. He stood before me in all his terrible majesty, so different from the boy. I snapped his picture. Twirling a cane chair, he smashed it to the floor.

In the gray dawn, he asked the girls who work for me if *they'd* led me to the barn. But he wouldn't ask the men, not for two or three hours. Then finally he grew distracted and marched them outside, too. In the mysterious tracks in the snow, he made them try their boots. When one's boots were too small, he signalled another to step forward. He cursed them: this man's and that were too small, too wide, too narrow, never quite a true fit. And all this time the boy remained upstairs with Signe. Who knows what they were doing?

Among the whores and hangers-on, he was the one being Sammy trusted. So much so that when the flute player appeared arm in arm with Signe, my husband yelled out, "See now where he comes from? Signe's room! My time was closest! I bet it would be last night that he fell, didn't I? Wasn't I right? Do you all see I was right?" But there was something missing — the joy one would expect to hear in a lucky man's voice. By then Big Sammy must have been aware that some-one had also known the flesh of his wife, my own flesh, I, Lillian's.

Not thinking, I suppose, that the boy was the very same person, that thief of my affections, Sammy called him to his side. Promising him a share of the pro-fits, Big Sammy hugged him for never lying to him as the others so often did. Before them, the camp-hangers-on filed past, the boy examining their boots. He came up with nothing incriminating (how could he: the boot marks were his own). The boy then said, "These loggers, they're innocent, Sammy. Their boots don't fit here." At which time, assuming Sammy's anger would pass, the men dug into their pockets and threw down some money in the snow, a peace offering.

"Please, let us have something, a party with your winnings, Big Sammy," they said as they stood around the pile. They all tried to cheer him up. But no matter how Marcella's music filled the air nor how the men urged him, he wouldn't budge onto the dance floor of the Blue Rondo. Sammy wouldn't dance the Two-Step that morning. He'd never been a dancing man. Finally, so that they'd leave him alone, he sent someone to dance in his place. When I saw that precious flute player waltzing toward me, asking would I like to dance, I shook with secret joy.

Logger upon logger cut in after that, Eddie Mitchell, Sever Lunde, and all that time Sammy slouched in the corner of the room, fingering a tin of Red Man. That morning no one failed to court me. For once, I, Madame Lillian, was the only woman in the place who counted. If it would have kept on like that, if it only could have kept on.

Yet, soon after, when Big Sammy talked of burning the place, the boy slipped off into the forest. It was just as well. The mere possibility of my cheating on Big Sammy in my *amours* reduced him to madness. There was no telling whom his fists would thrash at such times. The others circled him and asked in the nicest voices, "What's the matter all of a sudden, Sammy?" But he wouldn't answer them, not a word. "Get away!" he hollered. He had a nervous habit of shaking his fists and falling to one knee when he was riled. So kneeling, he appeared praying for divine, or spiritual intervention, when in reality he was only searching for a way out of his problems. Practicality to him usually meant violence; he was no praying man. "Go out! Leave me!" he yelled to anyone who came close that day.

I was thinking it would probably take him a week to get the kerosene or the explosives he'd threatened us with. We could have fun with Marcella's gypsy fiddle and the boy coming in from the forest, I thought. "Think of how warm and comfortable the place will be," I told the others. They believed me. As Big Sammy rode out on horseback, the loggers and girls who stayed behind admitted they'd never had a better time. No one telling them how to behave now, they toasted each other's health and fed on the olykoeks in the cupboard. Eating, drinking, me with my boy flute player, we went on without closing our eyes, lest it be the sleep of drunken exhaustion. And I always woke to find him true to me. "Your eyes sparkle, your mouth is soft," he'd say and play me something on the flute, "Jul's Waltz" or something. We piled the grate with logs and laughed and danced in the Minnesota night. We decorated each other with rhubarb leaves and for the first time in days the boy learned new songs on the ebony flute. We of the Blue Rondo were never so happy. The snow squalls stopped; the moon peeked through. I added sprigs of thistle to his hair and holly to his lips, and with a roaring fire, we danced in the wind. "Come join this dance," he cried. "Come everyone to the center!"

But such nights continue only so long with desperate men on the prowl. In the Blue Rondo, the hangers-on sensed it. In a week and a half, the place quieted. When the venison suddenly gave out, no one would pour drinks or stir the bear stew over the fire. In twelve days, our laughter ceased. In thirteen, the place was deserted. Signe stole the ebony flute, Marcella pleaded another engagement, and the boy decided on a long and happy life at his sister's in Beaver Bay. In fourteen days, the cold returned. I could feel it gripping me terrifically about the waist and loins. It wouldn't let go. With no one around, how suddenly quiet the woods had become, how deathly still and quiet. I looked in rooms to find their beds unmade. Men and women and girls had travelled off in my wagons. They'd left no flute for my enjoyment, no horse for my escape, just a camera. I took pictures of rooms that grew steadily colder. In fifteen days, I was certain of his return. That day, as I least expected the noise of the wind in the pines, I spotted a shadow crouching in the snow among the trees. Was it not Big Sammy's, the shadow of one who'd returned to an empty house? I wondered. In sixteen days, only I was left — dim-eyed, frightened, waiting. I, Lillian, a widow of forty, peered through the view finder of my box camera at Big Sammy, who was somewhere below me in the frozen garden resting there on his haunches. I could make out only his shadow in the moonlight.

The weather snapped sharply downward. I stayed bundled before the fire in the dancehall, hearing waltzes of the past echo from the walls. There I waited for my husband's glorious entrance. On the seventeenth and eighteenth days, I kept the fire going, but hardly ate or slept. We'd dance a Two-Step across the sawdust floor when he returned. To calm my last moments, I imagined "Halla Trallen" or "Nikolina" would be echoing from the walls as I came forward to meet his fatal embrace. This was one dance he knew so well — The Revenger's ... what? ... waltz, polka? Then Sammy would have the ice palace all to himself. And he could wander its halls seeking an end to the curse of that enduring music, that echo of the flutes and fiddles of long ago. Where did it come from, the echo? Where was the source of the strange, haunting melody? he'd wonder — until he'd drive himself crazy thinking about it.

The nineteenth and twentieth days I passed before the fire. All this time his shadow fell across the moonlit snow when in the evenings I dared to look out. The weather went even colder, far down below zero. On such bitter-calm nights, I heard the river ice groan above the snap of burning pinewood in the fireplace. But on the twenty-third day, finally, thankfully, the weather climbed almost to freezing. Just like that, it broke. In the sunlight, ice melted and dripped from the eaves. Leaving the fire untended, I opened the door and walked out. In the garden, where in five months or so I'd plant potatoes and tend beans and lettuce, a beautiful, frozen figure crouched on one knee in the frost. His eyes glistened with cold. His mouth was partly open as though he'd tried shouting something to me or to the cold at the very moment it stole his spirit. You could almost hear him. But what was he saying? A message to me to stop the music? He'd come this far and couldn't quite get out the message, couldn't quite stumble the thirty steps to the door of the House of the Blue Rondo. I knew if I found a spot for him in the shade the pines made, I could enjoy his fragile, violent temper for a good long time yet before the return of spring.

A SPINSTER'S CONFESSION
REGARDING HER SORROWS

I HAVE PREPARED THE BREAD and cotton when the priest arrives a little after eight. He's said Mass at St. Bernard's and come over. We have coffee.

"Your house looks very nice," he says. "Do you live downstairs? Where's your sister?"

"In her bedroom." I can hear her up there shuffling things on the nightstand. "She takes medicine for an enlarged heart," I tell him. "She hasn't been downstairs in ten years."

"My heart can't take it," she says when we're half way up. "Tell him that too, Julia! I hear you coming."

I carry up the table with the candlesticks, the bread and cotton and leave it outside her door. I whisper to the priest how I've heard her stories so often I have to cut her off midway to save my own sanity. "This time she'll tell you how a nice young man broke her heart. But, Father, remember it's partly the medicine that confuses her. Everything's become jumbled up in her head."

Entering the room, he notices the picture of the Sacred Heart of Jesus. Then Luanna starts in exactly as I said she would.

"I know the one who broke my heart," she says.

Her nightstand is filled with pills and water glasses. Gray curls fall out from her nightcap. She wears her glasses, and the counterpane is pulled up and tucked under her arm. Her rosary hangs from the bedpost.

"Luanna, Father McCraw is here."

We're already beside her when she answers, "Come in!" She reaches for the priest's hands. "You must know I wanted the baby, Father McGraw."

"Luanna, it's McCraw," I say.

"Yes, McCraw. Now that you've seen an old lady in her nightcap, may I tell you something, McCraw?"

"Go on," the priest says. So she proceeds with her favorite story.

"The river's name, it's 'left-handed.' Do you know why we call it that?"

"Indians called it that," I say.

"Don't intrude, Julia," she says.

"But, Dear, I want to get you moving. Father McCraw doesn't have all morning," I say.

"Well, as they canoed in from the lake, the Indians saw a river on the left. 'Nemadji' means 'left-handed.' 'Onawe' means 'Awake, Beloved.' Those are the two words I know."

"In seminary, we studied Latin," the priest says.

"Hurry, Lu," I tell her. "Let's get to the point."

"Well, I have a rather startling story," she says. "I hope you'll believe it on faith, Father, as you believe in the Trinity on faith. If you're willing to, then believe me when I say that my dead child returned once, even opened his mouth, muttered in his sleep. He was a wonderful, silent, sleeping child, whose dreams no doubt were pleasant for him. Are you able to believe that human beings return to earth and sleep for months, even years?"

Father McCraw takes the chair by her bed. He doesn't seem the least startled by her story. Perhaps, then, his imagination is large enough for her, I think.

"This man who made me pregnant and broke my heart," Lu says, "between us, there'd been certain difficulties. He was stronger emotionally. I found out about my heart where the sidewalk ends at the edge of town. That's where he told me he was married and had a nice house. He was always one-up on me, this man, this lover. 'I was sure you were no denier,' I told him when it was all over. 'But I guess your marriage complicated matters for us. Such pain does happen, I see.'"

"Yes, I've seen it," says the priest.

"Now that we're so intimate, Father, do you want to know more disappointments I've suffered through, more crises of faith? It's easy to understand how they've occurred. Where was the confessor to hear what I'd done? My faith had deserted me. I was very much alone, so what could I do in turn but abandon my God?" She points to the picture of the Sacred Heart. "For me, it was either faith in Him or human love, and I chose what I needed at the moment. It was His heart or mine."

Now I bother my sister to interrupt *her*. "Take this and swallow. Here's water." She takes the pill directly from my hand, sips some water. "Too many pills!" she says.

Outside, the city buses roar down West Seventh Street; in the distance, horns and sirens blare warnings. The bright, dry morning is perfect for early spring. Everywhere children outdoors will be happy, I think. At the school-yard across the street, they laugh and run about frantically. The Sisters at St. Bernard's have them singing Easter songs a month early, songs which drift in through the window with the sun.

The priest helps Lu put down her glass. He smooths her pillow and guides her head back. "You know," he says. "life's events are pretty easily counted, I've come to see: four or five passionate moments to mark the years. I count my First Communion, Ordination and first Mass, my mother's death and two or three other important events as the sum of my life. Perhaps they've been fewer for you, but just as important. Is there anything else you must tell me?"

"No, Father."

"Then, Luanna, having heard your confession, that you have experienced a loss of faith, I want to say to you in Latin, *Ego te absolvo* ... Go and sin no more."

"Don't absolve me of anything yet, Father," she says. "The child lived in my womb fifteen weeks. Do you understand? The baby disappeared before it was born. Don't look for it out there on the playground. I have for years. My lover sat in the waiting room of a hotel, then excused himself to buy some winter pants. When he returned it was over. 'You could've sat with me,' I said. He unwrapped the new pants.

"In another hotel, I lay awake. He stayed a day on business, then went home to try on the pants again. Left to myself, I stared at the ceiling. It was raining outside. I guessed it would for a month. Now it had started raining through the ceiling. I lay on the bed in the rain which came in around the ceiling light, then spread to the corners until, finally, the whole ceiling was raining. But I rested. I was not so weak in the morning but sick and worried with what I'd done. That was the start of my incompleteness. The rain stopped but the thunder didn't. I lay on the wet bed, thinking. And where was he but home in his new pants as I lowered myself into the bathtub which had those claw feet on it. As I dreamt of my child in this mean hotel, I wept. Taking the train home, I made it in time for work the next day.

" 'You were crazy to think it'd work out. It was impractical,' he said when we met again.

" 'Angelo, Angelo,' I said, 'how often you deceived me'."

That happened to Luanna forty years ago, I think.

"Father, I do what I can to keep Lu's room fresh," I say. "In warm weather, I keep the windows open, though not too much. The sound of kids playing hurts her. She takes Inderal for her heart. Sometimes she has breathing problems. I used to keep fresh flowers in the room, didn't I, Lu, but they bothered your breathing, didn't they? Ten years is a long time to live in one room, Father, and not move about the house, so I do what I can. I bring up the radio or change the lampshade for day or evening use. She prefers the rose-colored one at night. I also keep her water glass full. This room, you'll see, has plain wallpaper. Sometimes I think patterned paper would give her more to look at."

I don't know how we've spent the hours, I think, but it's suddenly close to noon. We've all been sitting here, dreaming, Lu staring at the ceiling. The alarm clock's ticking must have softened the moment, calmed us down.

"Has she told you the story of the odd, wandering family?" I ask.

"No," Father says.

"I want to make sure she doesn't repeat herself the way she does with me."

"Please feel free to go on," Father McCraw says

"Well, let me begin for her," I say. "It's startling, a truly startling coincidence, but that very same week she lost her baby in the hotel room, another child came into her life. You'll never believe this, Father. It will take great faith to believe it. He was a member of a pious family of travellers who bowed their heads before they ate," I tell him. "Lu has told me so often how they'd taken a table at the place where she worked during the trouble in her life. Until the boy dropped a piece of bread or a biscuit from the table, they'd been eating quietly with no problems. 'You know better,' the man beside him said. Luanna and I presume it was the boy's father. Anyway, he slapped the child's wrist. The boy forgot to kiss the bread he'd picked up from the floor. You could see they were tired, Lu has always said, and that the man did not slap him in anger. The kid cried, then fell asleep on the man's shoulder. They were all tired."

"That boy renewed himself," Lu breaks in. "If you could've seen it, the love between them all ... how without fear he put his head on his father's shoulder. He knew where affection could be found. You could never count on me like that," Luanna says. Pulling back the curtain, she gazes out the window. "All of them but the boy got up when they were done. He rested his head against the back of the chair and slept. I whispered 'Awake, Beloved.' I couldn't look at him long, for I had to work in the kitchen. When I returned and he was there, it dawned on me —"

"Father McCraw, they'd paid and left," I say.

"Walked out?"

"Yes, certainly," says Lu. She seemed to be gathering strength from recalling it. "And he was a fine boy, Father. His hair was soft and brown. White down appeared at his temples. Though his face looked as if he'd known the world many years, there was nothing harsh about it. His lips were so smooth. His wise head bent forward like my own child's would have been if he was alive in me. Those rainy days — what had I done? It was hard believing my own baby had gone away. And now this ... Give me my pills, Julia!"

I do, Theolair, which she must take several times a day. Her difficulty breathing causes her heart to swell. Her poor heart works hard, the doctors say. To them everything's physical. But how do we know it's not bursting for other reasons?

The pill settled, she breathes normally again. She clears her throat, looks at the priest. "My losses grip me," she says. "Except for Julia, I have been alone for forty years. Just me, Julia and the Trinity, a different Trinity from the one you worship, I'm afraid, Father. That evening the sleeping child was abandoned I had to return to the kitchen. The other waitresses and some of the cooks huddled around him. Customers came by and gawked. Some of them touched his hands or his hair as he slept. It'd begun raining. Where was his family? I wondered. Could they have left one so helpless, so simple and helpless? Was my own unborn child dreaming of me in his loneliness? Was it coincidence they'd come so soon apart? Was it God's design?"

"Stop a minute, Lu," I tell her. "It was Christian of her to look after him so well while he was there in the restaurant, wasn't it, Father?"

"Yes, I think it was," the priest replies.

"And the faith she exercised watching over this ... sleeper, didn't it mitigate her own sin?"

"Perhaps."

"And you, Father, do you accept on faith that anyone could sleep this long?"

"Well, strange things happen in life, and we must have faith to find the truth of what is revealed to us. What harm is there believing somebody can sleep an hour or two in a restaurant? It's no question of spiritual faith."

"But that's just it! She says it was a *year*, not an hour."

"It puzzles me that here memory fails when I can remember all else," Luanna says. "He came so soon after my loss—that's maybe why I'm so confused about him, whether he stayed an hour, half-a-year, a year."

"It's okay," I say, trying to calm her. I look at the priest. But Lu starts in again. "Yes, perhaps winter and spring were short ... and summer never came, and there was no fall. Say that that year you could count autumn weather in minutes, then the snow fell. An hour, a year, what difference? Maybe to me a year was like an hour that time. You know how, when you look back, sometimes your entire life seems to have been no longer than a few ill-chosen moments. Well, why not this? Why couldn't this happen?" Lu asks.

She pauses a minute as if to collect her thoughts.

"They'd left him to my care," she says. "They'd extended their goodness by trusting someone who looked as though she'd allow no harm to visit a sleeping child. Do you see the irony? The boss of course thought it was great. His business doubled. People were coming in twice a night to look at the sleeping boy in the chair. I would wipe his face with a damp cloth and sit beside him when I wasn't busy. The boss was good that way. After hours I would try to hold the boy before I went home. Having looked after him when I could during the day, I'd go home long after midnight. I'd see his face looking out at me from cars parked in the rain. At home as I looked in the mirror, I'd see him over my shoulder in the corner, just sitting sleeping with his head bowed. In my sleep I saw him crying. When his mother finally did return she made nothing special of all this. 'It's happened before,' I remember her saying. 'We hope he hasn't been trouble.' She threw her coat around the boy's shoulders and guided him out of the restaurant. 'We hope he hasn't been trouble....' That and nothing more and they were gone."

Lu looks up, as if she hates to return from the comfort of dreams. Over the past forty years nothing has counted but her losses.

"So, Father, I set my clock to dream of resurrection — and withdrew. Though I continued to search the playground of St. Bernard's nothing came of it. Thankfully I didn't end up downstairs in the house. My heart couldn't take climbing up here to look out. I can see fine from here in this room." She points from her bed to the window and the children of St. Bernard's playing below on this sunny day in spring. "I keep looking for my son."

"It's important for her to look out," I say.

"You know," she says, "the town suits me fine. east-side streets are named west Seventh or west Cedar. Our street is. When they founded the town the roads laid down a half-mile from the first houses were west-side streets. But the town expanded from its origins, so what is now the east-side has old, west-side street numbers in place. How things pass me by, Father McCraw, how I'm stuck here on west Seventh! Forty years I've worshipped the wrong Trinity, a baby fifteen weeks in my womb, a sleeping boy of about twelve or thirteen, and I Luanna, a recluse now dying, who almost gave birth."

She is quiet a moment. At such times, the alarm's ticking seems louder than ever.

"There's talk of straightening the river," she says suddenly. "Next fall they'll straighten and lengthen it, making it a 'right-handed' river, if you can imagine that. To do so, they'll bring a bulldozer and barge upriver, then dredge a course for the river through the island into the bay."

"West-side streets are becoming east-side streets, too," says the priest to console her. "Everything is getting restored to how it was. We're expecting new days."

She looks around at us, at the sunlight on the curtain, at the painting on the wall. Our Blessed Jesus points to His heart, a very sacred heart. Much too big to be contained, it rises out of His garments in flames.

"No, he wasn't. No trouble at all," she begins again. "Quiet. Never troublesome, my child slept, dreamt the whole time with head bent forward, the wise look on his face. Such a baby you've never seen. I fed him raspberries, carried him in the rain, left him in the city. The sleeper, too. I remember the boy. If I set the clock on the bureau, Father, it'll be my time before long. I've lived long enough. I want to join the Trinity. Let me think that I was no denier and that somewhere that sleeping boy naps in a chair in the afternoon sun. Allow me to dream that my poor, sleeping son is still coming back the first hour I hear steam shovels down by the river. Please, dear God, allow me the deceptions I can summon now that I have faith."

"*Ego te absolvo*," the priest says again. He whispers to me, "Even if she is wrong, do you condemn the heart's last stirrings, Julia?"

"It's raining," Lu says. She's sighing.

"Hurry," Father says, "light the candles." Then I know. He begins his prayers. In the hall, I have the bread and salt, the six balls of cotton to annoint her with.

"*Confiteor Deo omnipotenti....*"

She joins him, "I confess to Almighty God, to Blessed Mary, ever Virgin, to Blessed Michael the Archangel, to Blessed John the Baptist, to the Holy Apostles Peter and Paul, and to all the Saints, that I have sinned exceedingly in thought, word and deed...."

"*Mea culpa, mea culpa, mea maxima culpa,*' he says as he strikes his breast "*Ideo precor beatam Mariam semper Virginem....*"

She follows him, "I beseech Blessed Mary, ever Virgin, Blessed Michael the Archangel, Blessed John the Baptist, the Holy Apostles Peter and Paul, and all the Saints, and you, Father, to pray for me."

"May almighty God have mercy on you, forgive you your sins, and bring you to life everlasting," he says. But she does not answer.

"My unborn child," she says after a moment. She tries taking the priest's hands. "Don't forget my baby-child. I won't leave him again."

But out on the playground, children's shrieks of joy drown her out, and we can't hear. They're so happy it's nice out.

"It makes the ceiling wet, the rain," Lu says louder, as though frantic now to get it out. "Don't leave him out there."

She seems to struggle with the rain we can't see. Across West Seventh, the Sisters of St. Bernard's ring the school bell. Children's voices pour in through the window with the sunlight. They are going into the building for the last time in Lu's life.

"He's drowning!"

Father uncovers her hands and feet. Then we hurry to bring in the table with the white linen cloth and accessories. He will give her the Last Rites. I stop a moment to adore the Sacred Heart. It bursts from Christ's garments, a heart too large for Its body and all in flames. He is showing It to us. What is Its message? What fits the heart's wonting? I can't make out what It is saying to us. When I look again, Lu's gone, her head has slipped forward to her chest, eyes gazing nowhere if not at her own broken heart. Perhaps now she has gone to join the sleeper and her very own son. I think how it doesn't matter if I close her eyes to the sunlight.

"Blessed is the Holy Trinity and undivided Unity," Father McCraw is saying. He stands riffling through the pages of his book for appropriate prayers. He cannot seem to give it up and prays well on toward three o'clock as though embarrassed about sending her away in the rain.

THE HAPPINESS FARM

He'd gone hungry for three weeks. What mattered was his wife's smile. He was making something of her. Her bed was evidence of that: it was littered with Powerhouse candy bars and empty bottles of Nehi.

In the mess she slept like a queen. A bib protected the front of her pink dress. Sky blue slippers hugged her feet. Like the rest of her, they were dirty around the edges. But no matter, I'm in love, thought Herman. When she is as healthy as pig or fowl, there'll be time for cleaning her up, he thought. At such times, he'd soothe her golden flesh with creams and ointments and pat it white with powder. That'd be a glorious day when his calloused fingers occupied her flesh.

To get her to the roof, he'd rented a winch. He would uncrank its steel cable and drop a leather seat in a loop at the end to her bedroom window. Each afternoon he unwound and wound the cable to hoist her onto a rooftop mattress where she rested awhile in the sun. Afterwards, he'd lower her into bed and bring her a plate or two of supper before leaving her to her dreams. Of late he'd begun sleeping outside. She could use the room. She was so thoroughly fleshy — so magnificently gifted in that way — that she was confined to bed once they'd parted. The way he slept, he'd never be able to hear her if she started whimpering for him, he thought.

During the day as she dozed on the roof or in her room, he'd clean up the smokehouse, sweep the rutting shed, or rake the hillside where, lately, he'd seen some kind of strange marks — the Mark of the Beast? he wondered. He'd sweep them from his mind. Again and again, a vision of his wife waving from the bed and giggling came back to him as he worked outside. He'd feed her Lord knows what —melons, meatballs, dumplings, doughnuts. Including the trips he made bringing her the Sears or the Boston Store catalogues — catalogues for the "ample" lady, for the "big or tall gal" — he'd be up and down a hundred times a day. He'd push her candy close to the bed. He'd wipe her nose and change her bib. But his heart wasn't in it. Dressing her for bed, he couldn't find it in him to kiss her heavy cheeks. Something had been bothering him lately.

Outside at night he would close his eyes and try to forget. But it was hopeless. There was too much wrong. After all his work was this what things were coming to? Was this how it would end — Annie laughing in the middle of the night and filling the leather cinch with her big be-hind for someone else? When he remembered how she'd cursed him once, he thought he could go upstairs and take her throat between his fingers, squeezing and squeezing until there was no life left in her.

He sat beneath a plum tree. The sky is as cold as her heart, he thought. The whippoorwill ceased crying; the moon went down. Valley and farm were quiet. Even the crickets had gone to bed. He listened to his pocket watch and dozed occasionally, thinking of Annie. Annette Hobson was her name. He'd met her in town where he'd gone to look over a new Feed and Seed Store. As he ate lunch in the park, he saw her coming. She was thinner then, but not *that* thin, Herm thought, chuckling to himself. Half-way across the park, she'd dropped her purse and couldn't retrieve it. No matter how she positioned her legs, tried to push in her stomach, or stretched her flabby pink fingers, she couldn't quite bend far enough. She stood there sighing, staring at the purse. She tried hooking it with a tree branch. But when the branch snapped, the purse fell open and scattered its contents. To Herman's amazement, it was stuffed with candy. Lucky Heart and Good and Plenty rolled around on the sidewalk; Peppermint Patties squatted in the grass, sunlight glinting from their foil wrappers.

"That gal's an eater," Herman remembered thinking. "Scuse me," he'd said. "It'd be my delight and pleasure to pick these up for you."

She giggled. When he missed one, she pointed her fingers to it hiding in some crabgrass. He flicked the ants from it, and, with a flourish and bow, handed it to her. Carefully unwrapping the foil, she devoured the pattie and several others. She then presented him her chocolate-and-peppermint-smudged fingers. Just like that the four patties were gone, Herman and Annie were together in the middle of the park, and she was offering her stubby fingers to a man she'd never seen before. Herm congratulated himself: he had a way with women, he thought.

He'd accepted her fingers. Then they had walked hand in hand to the shade of a park bench. Still in shock over his good fortune and not wishing to press his luck, he sat at the end of the bench to give her room. But Annie, dissatisfied with the arrangement, sat down with as much force as she could muster, the bench tilted toward her, and along with it slid the out-of-town visitor who'd come only to buy feed. That was long ago when he was free of doubt.

He didn't hear giggling for an hour or two. Then he recognized voices upstairs. Peering around the corner of the farmhouse, all he could see obliterating the light of the stars as it twisted one way then the other from the end of a cable was a shapeless form, a jumble of flesh in mid-air. He heard whispering, too — from the roof. It sounded like the poor man from Bluebird Farm, whom Herman had taken for such a dear friend. Herman had once bought a mule from him — now to find him stealing his wife from under his nose. When she touched down, Herman heard the neighbor whispering, "Annie, darlin', are you in tight?"

The man himself must have slid down the cable, for before Herman came to his senses, the night visitor was pushing away, Annie giggling at him. It was a mistake, thought Herman, pinching himself to see that he was awake. He went to her room, running his fingers over her bedsheets. All that was left were a few crumbs from her Powerhouse. He pursued the wheelbarrow bandit.

He spotted them going through the pasture out back. He could see Annie's pigtails. Her slippers dangled over either side of the wheelbarrow. Pushing his cargo was Harley Matters. He must have been carting her away for days, perhaps weeks, thought Herman. Harley strained to move her faster. Gripping the sides of the wheelbarrow, Annie leaned into the breeze. Round and round they went, kicking up so much dust that Herman lost sight of them. Time and again, Harley and his cargo-on-wheels remained out of reach until, finally, in one vain effort and when Herman least thought he'd see his wife again until the dust cleared, he caught Harley's shirttail.

"I ought to kill you both," he hollered, shoving Harley. In the wheelbarrow, Annie sneezed. Fanning the dusty air, she shook her head. Sweat dotted her face and dress. Herman reached for a boulder. He eyed the man in the dirt. Then he looked to the beautiful lady in the wheelbarrow whose chubby fingers toyed with some bauble or other the midnight lover had given her. Here I catch her and she don't even care, thought Herman. He sized her up and scratched his head. He kicked the wheelbarrow and gripped the handles. Flexing his muscles, he tried lifting her.

Harley sniffled into his shirt cuff. He was a handsome man, though uncomprehending most of the time, Herman thought. Sometimes a vacant smile flickered and died about the corner of his mouth. The shadow of Harley's straw hat — a shadow which usually covered this smile — also covered the blankness, the lack of sense or understanding that was evident in Harley's face. Harley didn't know how to present a smart face to the world. That's why his farm's a wasteland, Herman thought. At Herman's, apple orchards and cornfields grew rich and good; at Harley's, soybeans died in the summer heat and grackles roosted on plowbits in the field. Soon he'd go under, Herman thought. Long after sun-up, Herm had seen him sitting out, whittling a piece of cordwood, chair propped against the henhouse, when he should have been plowing.

"Hi-dee, Herman," Harley would say, so that Herman, fuming, would lower his head and hurry by. "Bet you got work to do over to your place and cain't visit a minute."

Hearing him, Herman would grow angrier by the minute. To think the lazy fool could just sit there as his crops went to seed and his house and barn deteriorated.   "No, I ain't got work. I got nothing to do but feed my wife!" he'd yell if pushed far enough.

Then there was the mule, which Herman one day led by rope from his neighbor's barn in payment for various items which he, Herman, had loaned the poor, stupid, handsome man over the years. Herman said he was "buying" back the mule in payment. But this hadn't set well with Harley.

Now, Herman was too busy to be thinking of Harley, mule or not.

Something new struck Herman's imagination. The wheelbarrow would look swell in the yard, he thought. He took a better grip of it; with an upward jerk lifting once, twice. The lady inside began giggling.

"Hey now, that's a farm-work implee-ment, the only thing with wheels I got in the world," Harley shouted. "You cain't go off there with my wheelbarrow, Herman!"

It was going to be a fine day, thought Herman. Breaking into a trot, guiding his treasure through the dust, he didn't hear his neighbor cussing. This was sure better than murder.

The sun bobbing merrily in the early morning sky, Herman, his wife, and the new wheelbarrow made it downhill into the yard. Here everything was different: healthy, happy hogs squealed in the mud as bottom-heavy fowl, waddling back and forth, clucked greetings to the newcomers. Here one day, Annie would be healthy and happy. For here everything grew big.

The ladder shaking, his face flushed, up he clambered to the roof. With Annie twisting side to side, Herman felt as though he'd hooked the weight of the ages on the end of the cable. But despite the difficulty, up she came, his cargo bobbing in the leather seat. Each time he tired, he would rest, then renew his efforts and raise her another few inches until she was outside her window.

Mopping his face, he climbed down the cable, placed his feet on a branch of the plum tree and climbed through the window. The walls were plastered with photos, on the floor lay a broken vase, its withered flowers strewn about. He plucked a wilted daisy from the floor and rummaged around for something to protect her from the sun. The wilted flower in her hair, she was the picture of contentment, thought Herman. When he brought up the subject of Harley, she giggled and hid her face in her hands. When he asked, had she been seeing him long, she shook her head from side to side.

Stretching himself out the window as far as possible, he helped to brighten her spirits by tickling her under the chin. He teased her so much she couldn't stop giggling. Later, in spite of her laughter and the flies buzzing his head, Herman cleared off a place on the bed, fluffed up the pillows and closed his eyes. Finally he could forget his troubles. She was his for good. There'd be no more worrying, no more chasing her. He'd restored her to her rightful place. She swung halfway to heaven. And Harley, he wouldn't be back after this, thought Herman. Where'd his snooping get him anyway?

Herman thought of the uncomprehending fool with the run-down farm. No business sense, thought Herm. And to think that after dark he'd come poking around the yard of a man who knew life! But what difference? thought Herman. Wasn't he, after all, one wheelbarrow, one donkey, and one heavenly lady richer? He remembered his and Annie's catalogues. "Full-Figured Femininity!" that's for me, he thought. It would teach the neighbor a lesson, too. When that fool Harley saw Herman raising his wife up and down on the winch in a victory salute, when he saw how much larger she was getting everyday, he'd think twice about meddling with successful farmers. As a sort of memorial, Herman thought of planting begonias around the wheelbarrow, or a day lily or two.

He thought of their wedding night — how he'd pushed two chairs together for her to sit down on. She was the only woman for him. He thought of his farm thriving in spite of the blight around it. Everything prospered here. Under his expert guidance, there was no room for the sickly or pale. These he weeded out. That was why the neighbor upset him so. He was like that, slightly diseased. It made Herman's skin crawl. But there was no need worrying anymore. Without so much as a wheelbarrow to his name, the neighbor'd have to quit farming. My neighbor's a weak, handsome, sunk-chested failure! Herman laughed.

Herm guessed he'd seen the last of him. Clean living prevailed. The spoils were his. He decided on a pineapple layer cake for Annie with cherries on top. He'd lower her to the ground and fan her with lilac branches. Then, leaving her to savor the sweet life, he'd launder her dirty pink dress in the creek. And if the neighbor came around for food or drink, he'd shoo him away.

Herman laughed when he thought of how the work farm was the next step for poor Harley Matters. He looked around and congratulated himself. His barn was full, his animals happy. He cracked his knuckles. Could it be, he wondered, that he'd slept so much of the morning away? He thought of how sweet a glass of water would be from *his* well. But he was too tired to budge. It was nice stretching out. He lay watching the plum tree shimmering in the breeze. He smelled clover, dill and lilac in the garden below. Everything was in place as he liked it. Annie's shadow silhouetted the bedroom wall; the strawberry plants swayed in the gentle breeze outside; and in the summer garden, tomatoes grew rich and ripe on the vine. Hadn't he earned it, he asked himself, hadn't he done a good morning's work chasing Annie, pitting the strength of his arm against his neighbor's? Hadn't he earned a rest?

For a moment, there was a stillness in the air. He enjoyed the sunlight beaming through the open window. Outside, from the lowliest barnyard hen right up to the three-hundred pound wife, his farm was vital and healthy. There was goodness here and life. Herman thought of calling his place "The Happiness Farm." Soon he'd be pouring twice as much feed, chickens and pigs would be eating without stopping, and the geese would be growing fatter by the minute.

HELLO FROM TURE

EVERY WINTER IN TWO HEART someone is caught after dark where he doesn't belong — in among the big firs or out along the frozen muskeg of the river. Around here idle wanderers had better be careful. You may have seen Big Ture's house. A picture of him straddling its peak where snow has yet to reach was sent over the country. The intention of the photo was to show how bad Two Heart's weather is. Here's Ture in fur parka waving to cameramen, who must have been on snowshoes in the garden, to get off his land. At first glance, all you see are gentle curls of smoke, behind Ture the weather vane, then the deep, gloomy woods. Yet staring hard, you may observe below the peak exactly where Ture's legs are split, a crude, wooden sign reading: "Hello from Ture, Helen, and _____." "Kruger" is the missing man's name. He died the winter the picture was taken, and Ture ripped down the third name from the sign. Earlier, he'd refused Kruger a doctor, so that after a month of passing blood, Kruger stopped trying to convince Ture of the seriousness of his condition. But enough of that. How Kruger came to live here is my story, for he was no one's relative and only for awhile a lover to Helen, who was Big Ture's sister.

Those days, men like Kruger came regularly through Two Heart. On Saturday nights, the three saloons — the Crow, the Red Wing, and Sever and Eddie's out on the highway — were full of them and their boasting. Walking down Silver Street was a risky, terrible business. That was when Kruger came to town. Where he'd been was a mystery. Where he was going no one dared ask. As far as we could tell, he hadn't been working nearby — not at the lumber firms hereabouts. No one forgot him once they'd seen Kruger either. It was crazy, as if one day he'd dropped in out of nowhere, as if he'd suddenly decided (for it was obvious by his ragged, dusty clothing he'd been travelling) that our town as well as anyplace could solve the problem of his teeth. He came ahead of a late September storm, groaning and clutching his jaw with one hand; with the other, swinging a gnarled hickory stick at anything within the province of his arm. Good people out of fear bolted their doors and pulled down their shades.

At the Red Wing he tried numbing his mouth. Lifting his glass ceilingward, he downed his snowshoe grog with an improvident gulp. This made him only beller louder. He rampaged his stick from side to side. He went for powders to the drugstore. When they wore off, he complained again, each time worse than before, so that it seemed nothing in the entire world could comfort him.

It was as if he were bedeviled the way he clutched the bar. He was not a large man. Ordinarily, carrying on like that, he wouldn't have lasted five minutes in the Red Wing before someone called him out. But oddly enough at times here the patrons have a genuine sympathy for wounded or suffering men — except Big Ture, who sympathizes with no one. And so Kruger was left alone. No one came near, afraid that whatever malignancy crumbled his teeth and made his gums bleed might be contagious. Because of him no one laughed, sang, or called the bartender, who stood agonizing among them.

All this time from a booth in the rear, Big Ture eyed these most unusual proceedings. Nobody noticed that he'd begun laughing to himself. That was the way it usually was, that Ture was left to himself in the Red Wing. Twice he'd been barred from entering, once for chewing a man's ear off in a fight; another time for pocketing change off the bar that did not belong to him. But he was always allowed back in a few weeks later. He was no one to fool with.

Now he sat brooding, laughing, and watching the spectacle of the newcomer. Behind the bar Otto poured snowshoe grog, while in the corner Mr. J.T. Rowell struck up with the concertina. One look from Ture silenced him. When Ture rose and sidled up to the stranger named Kruger, who by then had quite forgotten his pain and slumped half-over on the stool, the whole crowd pulled back. First, Ture gently relieved the stranger of the hickory stick; then, as if he were examining the teeth of some wild animal, reached up and with thumb and forefinger opened the man's mouth.

None but Ture would dare such a bold yet gentle action. When he steadied the sagging head and opened the upper lip, hanging there, chipped and jagged, was a row of rotted teeth. No one had seen anything like it. Nor was the stranger very old. Something else had rotted his teeth. Under his sooty face which looked as if it hadn't been washed in months were eyes which only now, in spite of the snowshoe grog and the pain, were beginning to tire and lose their youthful flash, lips only slightly bruised. Yet something had gone wrong in his face. Ture lowered the stranger's head and helped him off the stool.

Ture's adventure in the Red Wing caused more than mild tremors in Two Heart. Not that it was such an unusual show, for there'd been other times he'd displayed such courage. But those were as quickly forgotten when he attacked the preacher with his fists or shot twin holes in Ed Hollister's boots. Ture was nothing for a town to be proud of. He had a stealthy mind. His problem was one of railing against the universe and smashing the nearest object with his fists when he saw he was going to be thwarted. Sometimes such furious shouting worked in his favor. More than once it had stopped neighbors from firing point blank into pigpens where, trapped, he stood bloodying his hands on the gate. "Look! It's Ture," they'd say at the last minute and retreat fearfully into the house.

Before the stranger came along, Two Heart had tried its best to leave Big Ture alone. For a time, in fact, a person was able to drink in the Crow and Red Wing without keeping an eye out for its least celebrated inhabitant. It seemed they'd broken Ture, and men went around congratulating one another in whispers. More and more the shades were left up when he passed by. Maybe he's more high-spirited than most, people would say, seeking to forgive him.

That was until Ture stole the train. Something got into him, and one night he made Ham Eudin's logging run to Bois Brule with the locomotive, leaving it idling at the reservoir crossing where he fell dead drunk in a ditch. After that he was more surly than ever. After what they did to him, he refused even to go to Sever and Eddie's on the highway. Out beyond the town they'd taken him and lashed him with rawhide until his face was roped with blood, then they telephoned Helen to come get him, having left a note pinned to his underwear that said, "I will not steal Ham Eudin's 8:52, as he needs it for work!"

But it seemed once Preacher Grove denounced him and the window shades again remained permanently drawn in Two Heart, there was less cause than ever for fear because, miraculously, Ture stopped coming to town. Even after he'd sufficiently recuperated and there was only a slight scar above his eye to remind him of what happened, he stayed away. At the Red Wing, Otto swore up and down. "This time we've turned him," he said.

While out in the cabin by the firs, Big Ture was biding his time. He was licking his wounds much as an animal will, only with the added benefit of his sister Helen's expert nursing and the oil of several antiseptics which she painted in red swathes across his neck and shoulders. Then the woods shuddered with his curses, and it seemed he would explode with hate.

There is a popular misconception of what hatred does to a man. With Ture it did not do what, according to this myth, it is supposed to do. He didn't wither under its burden. On the contrary, he grew tall and powerful so that once his back fully healed, once he was able to get around again, he disposed of his chores with a facility he'd never known before. And all the while he avoided the town.

His hatred, directed against Two Heart in general from the mayor down to the Indian mission's venereal sacristan, was wild and unreasoning. If Ture had a very difficult job, he'd add to the poison in his mind by avoiding the sensible approach. In that way he sweated and grunted, lugging hay by the armful up a ladder rather than pitching it or raising it to the loft with the pulley. And in the evenings instead of resting from his labors, he'd walk among thorns by the river.

When he'd been gone from Two Heart six months, he had to see those who'd caused his exile. For the occasion, Ture honed his knife. He could split a sheet of paper with its shiny blade. Moreover, he'd practiced throwing such a knife, so that his precision was uncanny. From as far as twenty feet he could throw accurately. He tucked the knife in his belt and pulled on his heavy shirt one late September day when a storm threatened.

That autumn Ture came to town with the storm rumbling in his ears, shining in his eyes. With his flying fists, he pummeled a bag of rice he had swinging from the barn rafters. He ripped the bag so wide that its contents spilled before him in a steady, white stream. He raced the storm to Two Heart, and all along he had to keep himself from shrieking. He could feel the cold knife steel press his belly as he ran, but it was other hurt and pain that kept him coming.

The Red Wing's volume of business increases substantially on Saturday afternoons so that there will always be men like J.T. Rowell who don't know of Big Ture. One reason for J.T.'s ignorance was that he's deaf; another, that he'd come to town after Ture'd been forgotten, disposed of by mayor and city council. J.T., who advertised himself as "The One Man Band," did not know enough to stop his foolish playing when Ture slammed open the door.

At his feet, J.T. places a small, cardboard placard, which says: "The One Man Band wishes you all a long, healthy, and happy life. Good Luck! And keep Smiling." This placard Ture kicked out of the way. Undaunted, J.T. began again, playing five musical instruments at once, each of which Ture noticed and reserved a great disrespectful laugh for. First, he laughed at the harmonica J.T. had wired around his neck, then he laughed at the battered concertina J.T. squeezed with his trembling fingers. On one leg this travelling musician keeps time with a tambourine and a cheap, tarnished cymbal, the tambourine fastened with bits of rope to his knee, the cymbal to the bottom of his shoe. With each tap of the foot comes a metallic sound harsh enough to drive weaker men from the room. With his other leg, J.T. beats tattoo on a bass drum.

Ture examined all of this while J.T. opened with a schottische. And when it became too much, Ture ended it by raising his boot heel so high off the floor he could hurtle it down like Thor's hammer at J.T.'s foot, so that the cymbal gave one final crash and J.T. fell atop his instruments. Ture didn't like the music.

He made his way to the end booth. From there he scanned the crowd. At once they returned to their beer, as if in their collective strength confident enough to overlook such minor distractions. Still, the men close to Big Ture shuffled in the direction of the wooden door through which he'd lately slammed. At last he has come for revenge, they thought. Now see how he does us in.

But Ture was content. He ordered one beer, then another, and another without incident. Satisfied that he had drunk his fill of beer, he called for whiskey, easing down a half-pint in no time at all. Otto began to fear for his exotic bottled goods behind the bar. If Ture raised something to throw, what would the bartender Otto ever do?

An hour passed. Ture soaked up his whiskey. He bothered no one. Along with his expertise with a knife, this patience was something else Ture had cultivated during his absence from town. Where before anything would provoke him, now he sat smiling, for all outward appearances content with the universe. Except for his knees, Ture presented a composed exterior.

But these he could not control. As his hatred smouldered, bursting occasionally into open flame, his knees jerked against the tabletop. As the afternoon wore on, they beat louder and louder. Try as he would he could do nothing about them. Each time he thrust the knees up was louder than the last, and the wall shook where the oaken top joined it. Gradually, the men in the bar began to notice this banging. But it was too late. For several hours, Ture'd been simmering, feeding his hatred with whiskey and beer. Finally, he could no longer wait. He grapped two bottles and ripped their necks off. One last time his knees jerked up, this time so powerfully they pulled the tabletop clean from the wall. For a moment it balanced neatly on his lap.

It was then, just as Ture was rising to do battle, that the peculiar visitor with the hickory stick burst in, crying and holding his jaw for all the world as if he were dying. Ture was dumbstruck. He'd seen nothing like it. He sat down, marvelling at how loud the man yelled with pain. For awhile he almost forgot his hatred. He stared and stared at the newcomer. Here was a man, thought Big Ture, who understood pain. Here was someone like himself. He was absolutely certain of it.

It did not take long to bundle the newcomer off. As the storm rattled around them, Ture limped under the stranger's weight. In the midst of the lightning, it began to snow. It continued that way until after dark when Helen unhooked the door and slipped quietly around back to the hogpen where she flung the peculiar contents of her pail. On her apron she wiped her bloody hands and left the pail in the snow. Later, the house became silent. The light in the attic went out.

So that's how Kruger arrived in Two Heart, a lumber town in the far north. For two days he chewed nothing but rags, swallowing his blood. He lived with only chicken broth and water on his stomach. The weight he lost cast his startling features into greater relief. He was much younger than Ture'd suspected. Once the soot and grime were washed off, it was clear that here, despite his airy gums, was a look that Ture had seen only once and Helen never. In his features, he was nothing like Ture. His hair was light as a wheat shock. His lips, still bruised from pain and Ture's prying fingers, were just now regaining the redness that Helen knew if it kept on would in one week's time be as deep as wild strawberries. His eyes were ice blue. That frightened Helen sometimes. Once in Buffalo Ture had seen a boy like that and followed him all over the docks.

For a few weeks Ture and Helen did not press him about where he'd been. It was enough that he rested. One could already see the changes he'd wrought in the household. Ture put aside his all-consuming hatred of Two Heart; Helen kept the place picked up. Sometimes she forgot herself and wore her hair about her shoulders so that at certain moments she looked almost youthful, her crazy, hawk-like features tempered by the firelight. Together the three of them sat in the shadows, Kruger nursing blistered gums, Ture sipping corn whiskey, Helen curling her hair about her fingertips. In that way they came to hear the story of Kruger's eluding the proper authorities of the State of Missouri and, crazed and half-drunk with pain and whiskey, showing up here one day with nothing but aching teeth, a hickory stick, and, as if by way of introduction, the sullen autumn clouds which dumped a foot of snow on Two Heart before leaving.

This is what he told them: in Sedalia once he'd come upon a hobo. For sport Kruger had armed himself with pebbles. Climbing a bluff, he began tormenting the hobo. First, he dropped a pebble into the river nearby, then a pebble onto the land dangerously close to the hobo's head. Soon the old man rose up, peered about, scratched his nose, and curling about himself like an animal, fell back to sleep. At which time — plink, plink, — Kruger began dropping pebbles into the river or onto the sand near the hobo's head. No amount of splashing could wake him, however. For now, dimly aware that someone was baiting him, the hobo decided to ignore whoever it was, leaving Kruger on the bluff in the afternoon sun with nothing to amuse him. This time, though, Kruger found something even larger to roll downhill. He found the boulder beneath a log. Rolling down the bluff, the boulder, because it was so large, stalled momentarily, regained its momentum, then proceeded on its way.

Robbing him of a wrinkled dollar and his few pennies, Kruger ran off and hid in the Sedalia freight yards. Then on the way north something very curious happened. It was as if by magic that first his gums began to fester, then his mouth to blacken, as if he were cursed with some pestilence, some grave, rotting abscess. Who can explain it? And yet this penance, this visitation, call it what you will, was something which solved a major problem in Kruger's young life, the one thing that had disquieted him over the years. Rambling north, he'd made the amazing discovery that the sore and painful mouth was far worse than what he had done to the old hobo. If this is so, then I can do anything, he thought. The pain is not as bad as I thought pain could be.

When Kruger finished, the hearth-fire dwindled. Immediately, Ture promised him a set of false teeth. Though Kruger said it was out of the question, Ture wouldn't hear otherwise. "You'll need your strength," he said. He coaxed Kruger into the shed where he'd kept moist a handful of clay waiting for Kruger's swelling gums to subside. He'd shaped the red clay into two horseshoes approximately the size of Kruger's upper and lower gums. He made Kruger bite firmly into one horseshoe, then the other. This done, he built a fire, melting a strip of plastic over it. With so little regard for the town, Ture had come to rely on his own ingenuity. He set himself to making teeth. He allowed the plastic to cool and set in the horseshoe molds of Kruger's mouth. In less than a week he would have the teeth themselves from town. They'd make the difference, said Ture.

But try as he would, Kruger's new teeth did not fit. Hour upon hour, Ture worked with them, filed them here and there, but when he put them back in they were always the same. The upper teeth protruded, making Kruger look as if he were laughing. Although they felt right, they looked funny, none of which bothered Kruger much, who saw it as a fulfillment of a theory he had divined in the box car — that he had to suffer at least a little for the pleasure he had in life. I look the same as ever, don't I? he thought to himself and clicked his new teeth together in front of the mirror, though Ture did not think so.

Nevertheless, Ture was happy. He saw Kruger in an almost mystical light. As far as Ture was concerned, Kruger could do no wrong. In fact, Ture started formulating ways to see if his visitor was truly holy, for the more Ture dwelt on Kruger's mysterious arrival, the more he was convinced that he was no mere straggler in the north, no runaway from the Sedalia authorities. What was amazing was the way the newcomer had with magic, the way he could make nickles disappear when right there only seconds before Ture had seen them between his visitor's fingers. It was baffling. Here, thought Ture, is a very wise man sent to rectify the pain I've felt in Two Heart

And so the two, Ture and the wizard-like Kruger, spent winter evenings prowling Two Heart's back alleys, sometimes probing windows to see if they'd give. Strolling back along the road, Ture would tell Kruger how the town had brutalized him. He told him of the night he'd been strung up and whipped bloody for Helen to find; how Helen had cut him down, pulling him home delirious in her vegetable wagon. That night, because she was all he had, Ture'd spoken to Helen of things he should not have, of things which were better left unsaid. When the newcomer heard how Ture had been treated, he promised the time was not long off when he should have his just revenge. This satisfied Ture that his visitor was genuine. From then on, with clenched fists and angry heart, he awaited Armageddon.

In those days, the two of them throwing themselves around, Ture's home was never quiet. Helen found her solace in apples, paring a winter's barrel in less than a week. And all along Ture and Kruger continued to go to town, careful each night to hide their tracks in retreat along the road. At times so eager was Kruger that he startled Ture, who at least had a reason for what he was planning in town. But what reason had Kruger? Whatever the case, Ture encouraged Kruger's violence. He never imagined that he'd have such a partner. All through December they were together — in the shed, the barn, the attic. Intermittently during the day, Helen would look up from her sewing to see them adjusting the bicycle wheel or shoveling their way from house to road. Once she'd surprised them in the root cellar where Kruger was doing something magical with five nickles he'd stolen from Helen's purse.

That month the snow was upsetting. She could count on two to four inches daily as much as she could on seeing Ture and Kruger heading to the bar. Each day as she made their supper, she watched the snow drift higher up the side of the house, so that she thought if they did not do something pretty soon she would go mad. Funny how this year she could not face up to working by candlelight at mid-day. That was what was going to happen, too; if they did not do something about the way they acted and the deep snow outside the window, she would go crazy.

One particularly blustery day not long after she'd begun having trouble with her sleep, Ture and Kruger left her and set off through the drifts in the direction of the river. Ture had the shotgun propped over his shoulder while behind him trudged Kruger with a sled, an old wooden milkbox affixed to the top of it. That was the day the snow finally covered the windows, when Ture and Kruger returned arm in arm through the storm drunk. With the milkbox full of squirrels, they'd returned from the hunting trip.

Where have you been? she asked.

See what we have in the box, said Ture. He motioned as if she were not even there. He stood silently, formulating his plans. In this box of squirrels, he had brought his sister something of value from the forest, a miniature cradle carved out of pine. She found it wrapped in waxed paper under the first layers of bloody fur.

By then it was early evening.

At that time of year it is especially hard if you are old and should be caught out late, as is evidenced by the couple who froze to death on their way home from the parlors of the Church of Two Heart. But as the days passed before this night when at the stroke of twelve Ture took his revenge, both he and Kruger had become used to the cold, so that each degree the thermometer plunged succeeded only in bringing a ruddier glow to their faces. Whenever Big Ture heard ice snapping in the river, his pace quickened with anticipation and Kruger appeared to be smiling within the outline of fur that surrounded his face. They were going to town this very night and be done with it.

After a brisk hike among the trees, they spotted the town, stiff and brittle in the night. Ture's heart beat wildly. When Big Ture raised the clawhammer the first time, frost spread its way over the glass panes. In a moment the window of the Two Heart Cheese Shop shattered, its pieces flying across the floor, some as far back as the cooler where special wedges of Swiss and Colby are kept. Swinging the clawhammer, Ture smashed the window of the Red Wing next, as if here were concentrated all the sorrow and disorder in his life. Building to building he ran, kicking out windows, sliding the clawhammer across everything that broke, so that in those few moments, reeling with the rare and heady atmosphere of the just, Ture found true happiness. He eyed Kruger, Big Kruger, setting a fire. He longed to be with him in the ring of flames. The fire leapt from building to building, from the Red Wing to the Cheese Shop to the cafe and all down the street.

Pumping his hands up and down, Ture roared to the heavens. He patted his partner and slapped his partner's shoulders, and Big Ture grinned at the quarter moon above. Together outside in the brisk air, Ture and Kruger could smell woodsmoke and hear the river's restless snapping. Kruger cupped his hands together. He made a filthy gesture. It was as much to say: if the town is a woman, this is what we've done to her. And Ture clapped with joy. He laughed so hard his belly ached, and he stumbled back along the road leading home.

In no time, they were safe in the house, their heavy boots steaming before the fireplace. While Kruger entertained his host, Helen mixed them whiskey and lemon drinks. They laughed so that actual tears streamed down Ture's face. This time with his hands and the shifting firelight, Kruger cast shadows upon the wall. It was a crude portrayal of the love-act. He had never seen this side of Kruger's talents. He enjoyed it thoroughly and when Helen left the room, he asked for more of the same. So curious was Ture that he followed Kruger's fingers with his own in an effort to find the secret of his art.

Shortly afterward, worn with the excitement of the raid, Ture had given in and fallen asleep at the table, his hands around a bottle. Then something unfortunate occurred in this house by the firs. No shots rang out, no posse banged the door, but in its own way what happened disturbed the forest calm just as surely. It came about as Kruger appeared to be napping contentedly by the fireplace and after Helen had said her good-nights. It was then Ture felt it strangling upwards. He saw at first through bleary, half-closed eyes the fire no longer silhouetting Kruger, the chair empty by the fire. With a great, wild gasp, Ture rose up and pulled the air deep into his lungs, emitting as savage a cry as had ever echoed within those walls. That somehow Kruger had up and gone away in the night, leaving him forever, was what Ture had thought, and it drove him frantic. He beat his hands against his mouth and pounded his fist into his palm — all before he thought enough to see which way Kruger's tracks led from the house. Finally, he threw open the door. Awaiting him were the firs and the snowed-in path. There were no tracks. So he hasn't left, thought Ture.

When it finally came to him, he could do nothing more than rock by the fireplace. How long it had been going on, he would not ask them. A hundred plans crossed his mind. As the sun rose, he had all he could do to keep from shooting her. He oiled the shotgun and sat rocking by the fireplace. Finally, he arose and prepared his own oatmeal so Helen would not have to do it.

In the morning Helen and Kruger came to breakfast as if nothing had happened. While she readied the coffee, Ture eyed Kruger across the table. Ture did not let on that he'd seen his shameless sister caught in the love-act. On the other hand, Kruger, the wizard, was like a man come upon good fortune. He guzzled his breakfast, while Big Ture sat staring over the top of his steaming coffee. Kruger asked him, didn't he like his eggs? Wasn't Helen's cooking just fine? Kruger asked Ture then if he wouldn't like to scout around town and pick up the news. And all the time Ture wished that it had never happened, for before Kruger had been so perfect. His face had healed now from when he'd come in September, and his hair was as light as ever. Ture's heart was broken. No, I have work to do here, but you go, he said. He belched. Take the bicycle why don't you?

As soon as he left, Ture aimed the shotgun at Helen. She sat in the corner where Ture had flung her. She was sobbing, head between her legs, but he called to her in a soothing, brotherly voice. Helen, my dear, he whispered. He trained the twin barrels at her eyes. That was when the idea of the burning came to him. Please, Ture, let me go to the bathroom. I'm going to be sick, Helen pleaded. Go right there on the floor, I am going to burn down the place anyway, Ture replied.

Brother and sister sat in the kitchen. Twice, Big Ture walked over and made her place the shotgun barrels in her mouth. He said she was defiled. Then they heard Kruger stomping his boots out on the porch. Ture held back the curtains, smiled, and waved for him to come in. Ture hid behind the door when Kruger wiggled the handle and called out. "Well, I'm glad to see you're feeling better, Big Ture." That was when Ture whacked the back of Kruger's head with the butt of the shotgun, so that Kruger's false teeth flew clear across the kitchen, landing in the frying pan. Stunned, Kruger went to his knees. He shook his head and gripped the table. He rose up slowly. Ture aimed for the broken buttons of Kruger's coat. When the butt of the gun hit his chest, Kruger sounded as though he were exploding. Ture hit him again. This time Kruger collapsed without Ture's having wasted a single shell.

With Helen sobbing in the corner, Ture had all he could do to keep his head clear. He warned her once. When she continued, more hysterical than ever, he bent her arm back, which quieted her for a moment. But he didn't burn the house down. Instead he dragged Kruger's limp body into the living room, propping it half on the couch. The false teeth he left in the frying pan.

The next few days, in spite of her aching arm, Helen did the best she could nursing Kruger. In view of their limited medical supplies, this consisted of applying an occasional ice pack to the base of the skull where purple swelling had appeared as a result of the blow from Ture's shotgun. To Helen it was clear Kruger had suffered internal injury, for although he was awake, even given to muttering a few words when he was sure Ture had gone out, he was unable to get up, nor could he stop himself from coughing up a sticky mass of blood every few hours. Helen could not stand to look at it. When he was expecting a coughing jag, Kruger would signal her so she could run into the kitchen.

Through this trying period, Big Ture kept mostly to himself, as he was wont to do before he'd met this stranger. He stalked the forest and roamed the farm. One morning, unusually receptive to the cold, he marched to the river, cleaned a space, and donned his ice skates for a whirl downstream. And all this time, Kruger was dying inchmeal. When Ture came by eating a cookie on his way upstairs to the attic, Kruger began asking him if he wouldn't, please, get him to a doctor. It was all he could do to mumble these words and, like magic, blood appeared at the corners of his mouth. Ture did not hear a word, though, and day by day Kruger sank lower. After a month, his face was turned into parchment and bone. This may be another of his tricks, thought Big Ture when finally, and for the very last time, Kruger implored him to seek a doctor. Bring back a doctor, please, Ture, he said. And Ture said no. Then at least give me my teeth back, Kruger pleaded. But they remained where they were since the morning Ture surprised Kruger from behind the kitchen door.

But what is most unusual about this whole affair is not whether Ture heeded his partner and gave Kruger his teeth, but instead how Helen changed in the days following the assault and how she came to make Brunswick stew, for that was Ture's favorite. It was she who astonished Ture. In the end Kruger lost his will to live. A day or two this side or that could not have made much difference.

When Helen saw Kruger's condition worsening and that any day he might die, she began thinking of herself and where she stood with Big Ture. Her brother refused to talk to her. He wandered in and out and sat down to table, but talk he would not, which worried Helen. She wondered what he would do to her once the visitor was gone. Although she thought Big Ture would let her stay on, she could never be sure, just as she had learned never to trust completely the behavior of wild forest things, dead squirrels in the milkbox. And so she made up her mind, and because Ture was stronger, she decided to ignore Kruger, who was beyond help anyway. All day he lay snivelling on the couch, coughing into his hands, and after a while she forgot to change the nightshirt which became encrusted with blood.

Her new station, however, was the kitchen. The cooking smells emanating from that room, with its huge oven, were enough to bring Big Ture indoors hours beforehand even on the warmest winter days, when the temperatures reached zero and only three inches of snow were predicted before nightfall. The smells were tantalizing, and when Helen baked one of his favorites, Ture stood sheepishly in the doorway. Once it was Northern pike and once it was Applehead pie. Ture liked his pie steaming hot — on top a slice of cheese or a scoop of ice cream, which he himself churned in the barn. The first day he had the pie he hollered to Kruger, "wouldn't a wedge go swell right now?" But it had been at least several days since Helen attended Kruger, and he hardly had the strength to raise his voice and ask Ture to please get him to the doctor quick.

Then he fell silent, and when Big Ture wandered by sipping some delicacy or another which Helen had painstakingly prepared, though not the Brunswick stew to which she was building gradually, Kruger stared up questioningly from the hollow of the couch, his skin burning with fever. In the days since he'd fallen prey to the butt of Ture's shotgun, Kruger's face wrinkled horribly. It was especially like this about the mouth where, in spite of the missing teeth which Ture in a moment of beneficence had returned to him, the skin was taut, rough, and gullied with ugly seams. The teeth served only to heighten the comedy of Kruger's face.

But Helen had no time for him now. Kruger's life would have to run its course, she thought, for she was too busy in the kitchen. She was making a stew for her brother the likes of which he'd never forget. That Kruger should die on the afternoon of the stew, that his eyes should roll up and a ghastly breath escape his lungs as brother and sister sat down to their first amicable meal in weeks, was only coincidence.

There were five pounds of chicken in the stew, because that is how Ture liked it. There were also heaps of lima beans, several ripe tomatoes, and a handful of salt. Coming in for the first time that afternoon, a smile crossed Big Ture's face. He sniffed the air and clapped his hands. What are we having? he asked. Something, one of your favorites, Helen said. Taking her by the hand, he guided her into the next room where Kruger lay straining up with dull and glassy eyes at them both. Ture told him how Helen made a Brunswick stew, how life was not so bad after all. Can't you just smell the stew? he asked.

ICE DAYS

The sack hung about Paul's neck. He stood at the edge of the clearing. "Over here, Gunnar! How's your mother?" he asked.

"She complains of the cold," Gunnar said.

"And you?" asked Paul.

"I've no complaints. How would my getting cold look?"

"If I were cold, I wouldn't admit it either," said Paul as Gunnar hurried past him through the thicket into the wind. Gunnar thought, *The cold has taken him. Paul wanders the cold frozen with sin. He's too far from the sun.*

Thinking how you could guide yourself by the cross on the roof, Gunnar headed toward his home, which was built deliberately to face the cardinal points so you couldn't stray.

Wandering, I'm still not lost, not with the cross to guide me. One can pray and mend one's ways. The owls, wolves and bobcats are lost. Paul with the sack about his neck, the others, the hundreds of others, yes, they are all treacherous, evil, mean-spirited sinners consumed. But me? No.

In the failing light, he made it home. The wooden cross looked somber against the sky. There were paths to the strange places where dead spirits stood. At night the air filled with the smoke of fires which didn't warm them. *The stinging night offers them nothing,* thought Gunnar. *There is little consolation in the eternal winter of this cold, dark place, only the snow drifting about the shelter's eaves on St. Lucia's night.*

Despite others available to him, Gunnar broke a new path to avoid the cardinal points. The cardinal points were good points from which lost, wandering souls could learn — as they could from the crucifix. But you sometimes couldn't see East-West-South or North in the night, and sometimes the cross was merely a shadow. He'd done right, Gunnar told himself, to make a new path and to save for sinners the ones that approached from the cardinal points. That was the right thing.

"Gunnar!" she hollered and banged the alarm kettle with her hammer. She expects something, Gunnar thought. *A storm? her very own death? Is that what she's doing? Banging it away with an alarm kettle? Keeping her own death at arm's length? Is she out-banging the noise of her sins with that hammer, out-foxing the noise of that cold with those blankets, those walls? I'm doing right*

119

building her inward, for strong walls keep sin out, I was taught. Walls keep Syl Magda safe inside. My mother. Mine. Syl Magda. No sin, shame, strife shall enter here tonight. Nothing shall attach itself here.

She lay in bed complaining when he came in from the fine snow that had begun falling. When he told her, "the ice sparkles, will you come see it?" she banged out her answer on the hammer and kettle. When he said to her, "Mama, I'm going out shooting under the full risen moon," she wouldn't listen but kept banging at the kettle. "*Fader vår som är i himmeln,*" Gunnar prayed. Outside, the fox made off with the winter's chickens. It was a sad, strange thing all around.

"Do you hear it in the chimney?" she asked.

"No."

He was wearing the lighter coat. He'd succeeded in boarding up an inside window — not with the broken hammer he'd fixed and given back to her to bang the kettle with, but with the good, sturdy hammer.

"Sleep?" he asked.

"No, put more rags under the door. I'm cold," she said.

"More rags," said Gunnar.

Clutching the hammer, he went to work across the room where some fresh boards waited. He set to on the north wall. With the saw, nails, chisel, plane, the rule, the two hammers — one sturdy, the other broken — he did his work. He raised walls to shut Syl Magda in and keep her from cold. Outside, the world's sins and the cold wind, but inside the walls would keep her safe, warm, and quiet.

The pattern of the inner walls followed those of the outer. Already he'd raised beams and made a roof four feet below the original. The walls of the cabin: they were 30 X 35, the next room's 20 X 25. To keep her from evil, he'd built a house within a house, a cabin within a cabin, a prayer shelter within a prayer shelter. Then there was the newest room. Third, innermost, it stood another few feet in from the last one he'd built. He was working on it now.

Outside all these walls, the wind shook the treetops. In the new room, he caulked whatever holes or knots appeared in the boards. He'd built it with windows so that you could look right out through three prayer shelters — one inside (or outside) the next — to trees, to firs and white birches, trees of the night and winter time. But now he was boarding up these windows, not building or refurbishing the shelter and the windows, but boarding them up.

"Under the door there's a draft."

"Under which door?"

"I don't know. I'm mixed up," she said.

"There's nowhere else to move you. I'll come give up my coat."

He blew the sawdust away from where he was working, lay the coat gently on the four-post bed, which was wooden — handmade like everything else in there. Inside in the center, she lay, her bed raised on wooden blocks. On the

120

elevated bed, she was higher than he.

"The chimney, is he there?"

"No," said Gunnar.

The woodstove by her bed provided heat to the cabin. Dust and soot filtered down when he craned his neck up into the cold fireplace chimney. (There were three fireplaces in the cabin, too. He had laid stones for all of them. In every way the three fireplaces were identical.) He was busying himself inside the shelter now.

She was right. In the chimney darkness: there was something up there.

He opened the door, rushed the few feet to the next, and through that to the next. Outside it was a night where sin lived. He shielded his eyes against the moon, saw something above. Now the river heaved and dislodged its ice in patterns on the shore.

"Come down," he yelled.

He could barely hear his mother call. "Do you hear it in the chmney outside?"

He didn't answer, could hear her hammer against the night.

The wind swirled. He'd left open his heart. He raced to the door. The wind ripped his coat. Sweeping the snow away, he slammed the big door shut, slammed another.

"Stay in," she said as he slammed the last. "Don't go. This night help to keep me from trouble. I'm seventy-nine."

She's not seventy-nine. She's little more than fifty-four. He didn't know what made her talk so. He thought of leaving forever the innermost shelter with the raised bed in the center. There was too much to find out in the forest dark. Sometimes he watched the night wheel by. Dressed in furs down on the river, he thought how he'd never been part of the night, not like the beasts whose skins he wore. In this cold land he'd observed night and sin but neither embraced nor understood them. Sin and the night world he'd never understood.

He and Syl Magda, his mother, had travelled here long ago searching for Gunnar's father, who'd set out from Värmland. Gunnar's father had sailed N-NW, becoming trapped in the ice, at which time he'd stepped out upon the windrow and died. He did not die spiritually, however, not that way, for he was not a spiritual wanderer, but a good, honest man. Some peasants had sent him to the nearest village, which was named *Paradis* of all things — or *Djurgaard*. Finding Gunnar's father there on the northern ice, they'd sent him to *Paradis* and continued their own journeys looking, in sorrowful penitance, for loved ones who themselves had died, though in less desirable ways.

Gunnar was now twenty-two years in the Lord's service. Did one never quit? Coming north, he'd had no fear of being defiled. He'd never had cause to fear for his soul. "You can't and won't sin," they'd told him in the church as a child in Värmland. Over the years he'd prayed and kept lights in the prayer shelter's windows, lights in the night of death and sorrow. It was his mission. *I'm ministering to dead souls in this outpost of faith. I can teach them. Like Paul, the owl-man, they are doomed, but I can teach them why they wander.* He kept a light in the prayer shelter so that if they should look in, it would be on the workings of the prayerful family, the mother and son, Gunnar and Syl Magda Johannsen. *As the farmer reaps wheat, so must I, at such great distance from the sun, reap snow....*

"The chimney!" she yelled.

From the roof he heard cries. He didn't believe there was anyone out there. He stoked wood, added a log, went to bed. He was no part of the night world. He'd learned to sin, but in small ways. He'd felt neither terrible cold like her nor the night of sin. "There's no man up there," he yelled. "Nothing! No one."

Because he slept just outside the newest room (third, innermost), he found he must wear skins and furs to ward off the cold.

In the morning he sprang up. He went outside to check the prayer shelter. Then he hurried back in, shut the door, then the next. It was a bad morning, and it chilled him — but not with the chill of sin. Was his own good, holy mother possessed of the night and cold? he wondered, closing the last door.

She held out her hands.

He soothed her. "What is he like, Gunnar Johannsen?" she whispered.

"No one's out there, no thing, Mama," he said.

"Well, do you have to keep going out?" she asked.

"I can work inside on your room. Are you any warmer? It's bad."

"No warmer. Is he up there?"

"No one, no," Gunnar said.

"You're lying. He's coming down trying to get me. I think he's the cold heart of my nature."

She rolled over. He fed the stove.

"The draft's bad," she complained.

"I'll go to work on it. Didn't I say I would keep out the cold?"

He was a builder, a keeper of a lighthouse. He climbed up on the ladder to the third room's ceiling. Efficiently and without complaint, he did God's bidding. He was a listener, too. At twenty-seven years of age, he sought the woods to understand what he could from them. He did not understand his good mother's suffering a sinner's torments.

That blustery day he worked round her bed, her face looking like a hawk's ... a crow's, thought Gunnar. Her hands curled inside each other. She'd been that way a month. "The draft. Can you do something about it?" she begged.

"No, can *you* do something about it?"

He strung a line. He was touched with grief. Outside, people wandered. Perhaps I have brought cold into the house with me, he thought. Perhaps I am tainted with cold and coming unto her high, holy bed a sinner.

For only a minute she was without a blanket, long enough for him to run the rope line from one corner of the new prayer cabin to the other. Then he strung another line. When the ropes intersected, Gunnar moved her on the bed. The lines met over her belly, exactly there and she was centered. She was exactly as far from each corner. In the process she'd been blessed by the cross the ropes formed over her belly. He gave up a hearty thanks. Perhaps because of the sign of the cross formed by the rope she would be getting better, he thought. Perhaps that was what she needed.

The thing — it was an owl, a snowy owl with wings five feet across when it flew.

Going out, Gunnar carefully pulled rags from the bottom of each door, but replaced them carelessly on the outside. No doubt drafts would come in, he thought, but in the woods he couldn't hear a complaint anyway. To get away from here I can go as far as I choose, even out among the wolves and bobcats to learn of sin's cold, its grief.

When the moon was full bright, the crucifix threw its shadow from one bank of the river to the other. He made squares out of the moon's pattern on the snow. Kneeling in the center of the frozen river, he threw off his cap. One square held his coat; one his boots; one his cap; the last his belt and gloves. Each square contained him no less than a minute before he retrieved his items from the treacherous snow. Paul watched him the night of the eclipse; Paul, the owl who was an old man.

"What are you doing?" he'd said.

"Praying," Gunnar'd responded. "New prayers. Never-said-before prayers. Come here with me to the center of the square. These aren't conventional prayers."

"See how you've destroyed the shadow of the cross? I'm not sorry for you, Gunnar," Paul said.

After that, Gunnar'd gone home and driven his nails truer than before. Later that night, he knelt and prayed again that the snow make better sense to him. But Syl Magda called to him, interrupting his prayers.

Under the bright moon, Gunnar spotted the owl. It had been two days up there.

"Come down from our roof!" Gunnar hollered. "What do you want? No one's here!"

It fluttered around in the chimney. He was silent, the moon gone under when he closed the outer door.

Past midnight she started the hollering and banging. From the outer rooms he rushed to where she lay.

"What is it up there on the roof? What do I hear all the time?" she asked.

"There's no one up there," Gunnar said. "I saw no one."

"You saw —"

"I saw no one up there."

"You wouldn't notice my dark nature," his mother said. "Look at me ... my hands. Please light me a candle. Say prayers for my safe-keeping. Purge me with hyssop, son."

"Mama."

"I'm cold on this raised and centered bed now."

"I'll lower you."

"I know what he carries round his neck. See if he doesn't."

The light was dim. She complained to the crucifix over her bed. He prayed. She was silent, shaking.

"I can feel it," she said.

She was curling up on herself. Hands, arms, shoulders curling up.

"Father in heaven...." he prayed, *"helgat varde Ditt namn,"* then quit when he saw the owl's face in the window. Gunnar's mother thrashed about. He stoked the fire, bundled some furs over her. He went out of the shelter where she yelled from the elevated bed, went out, shut the inner door, opened the next, shut that, opened the next. Snow flew up. He edged around the corner. He was standing there facing Paul, who had the bag slung about his neck. Paul waved, gave the bag to Gunnar. The snow came between them, and he was gone.

Indoors, Syl Magda was still crying. She'd gotten so thin, so old. He loved her. He was like her more than anyone at that moment. He stepped into the prayer shelter.

"You saw him, Gunnar. Please talk to me about him. I will choke on my words if you don't talk."

Gunnar was silent. When she started in this time, her voice was higher.

"I'm sick of the cold," she said.

"It's much warmer in here," he said.

She was talking about a coldness of sin he'd never felt.

"How did I know it was part of my nature to do as I did?" she said. "That man out there who's trying to get in, he got a speck of something — soot, dust — in his eye once."

"Yes."

"I leaned over him, licked his eye in the old country way."

"With your tongue you licked his eye."

"I did lick his eye."

"And I was a baby in my chair, you said?"

"Yes. And this was in Värmland and your father had just set out to this mission place of dead souls. And this wasn't the one time that I licked his owl's eye. I willingly did so. You in your chair I turned to the wall and hummed a melody to calm you while he waited in the room's shadows. He looked ancient when a pine knot burst and threw sparks around his feet. By then your father was gone two months. Prayers to the Heavenly Father fell on deaf ears...."

Gunnar rose up, took the cross from over her bed.

"I'm sick. I'm sick, dying. I can feel the cold, Gunnar, I'm full of sin's cold. Please pray and protect me, Gunnar!"

"Please pray and protect you," he said.

He gathered the crucifix, the rope he'd made measurements with, some drawings. Syl Magda begged him not to take them away. She was weak, curled around the blankets.

"*I'm* sick," he said. "I'm the sick one."

In the window the face of a man whose fingers scratch away at perpetual frosts peered in. Gunnar saw from inside the room, could watch him right through the window. Gunnar carried the bag about his neck. There were the three of them in that desolate scene: Gunnar, Gunnar's mother, and that cold and ancient master. She was wild. She didn't know where she was.

"Rest," he said.

She tossed her head from side to side. In the next room, he prayed. Not for her, but for himself. She appeared to twist in half. Bent up, old, she hollered for him.

"Son! Son!"

"Mother! Mother!"

He was praying hard. He read the sign in the window frost, the same as he'd made in the river snow.

"We cut each other's hair. We kept it in a bag. We did that," she said from the other room, "each time he came over. We talked about it. How evil! When ice went out into the lake my hair was on the table in Värmland. We'd cut it short. There was some power we shared. It wasn't a good thing, Gunnar. I'm not sure what to think about it. I didn't know he died — now to show up, the dead man at my door. He reminds me of the coldness and treachery of sin."

"You're not sure what to think," Gunnar said. He himself was learning from the forest. He'd learned things out there. Because of his faith he was *just* learning. One thing was a new way to worship. *That is why — no longer alive to the warmth of prayer — spirits wander in death outside the window. Without warmth, without hope of light.*

He shut his eyes, tried not to shout when he opened the bag that hung round his neck.

"I'm dying!" she yelled.

"You're dying," he said.

"Cover me from the cold, Gunnar."

"Cover *me* from the cold, mother!"

He turned his head away and with a chair propped open the inner door. He kicked rags from the bottom, opened the next door, kicked those away, opened the next ... opened the entire shelter to the cold.

"Please help me," she said.

"Please help you," he said.

"I need some water now!"

"You need some water now."

He poured a cup from the dipper in the bucket. He dusted the surface with ash, handed her the cup.

"Thank you," she said.

"Yes. Thank me," he said.

In the other room, praying, he dressed for the forest cold. *"Jesu!"* he muttered on the way out.

Night trees caught his fur. He travelled through ash-dirtied snow to the gloomy places of the soul, observed others silhouetted against their fires. Gunnar saw the twi-lit sky.

She licked his eye when he had something in it. That was not the first time. Before father died, she consorted with souls whose cries now echo the smoke-filled sky and hang like slate-gray ribbons from the trees.

Night and cold claim their own. But I am the truly sick one. For I renounce my building inward and my narrow rooms, a narrowness which I thought would provide. I renounce her — Syl Magda. And because now she begs in the midst of pleading for water and more covers, I throw off her blankets and salt her water with ash.

He went deeper, removing the wolves fur where some hazel brush had caught it. He was their keeper and the single light in the forest. He walked through their fires and knew he was their guide. Then he heard someone calling from deeper in yet, a man who looked like an owl.

"This way, Gunnar, here! You were teaching me down there on the river. Can you believe such a thing? That *you* were teaching me? Down on the river where the crucifix was...."

Gunnar removed his heavy gloves. Now there was no fire. No light whatsoever brightened his face. A fierce crying off somewhere in the wilderness.

"Here, this way, Gunnar, this way where we no longer have to listen to her futile beating against the cold...."